GOING
VIRAL

Also by Katie Cicatelli-Kuc

Quarantine: A Love Story

GOING VIRAL

a
socially
distant
love
story

Katie Cicatelli-Kuc

Scholastic Inc.

Interior photo © Rabilbanimilbu/Shutterstock

All rights reserved. Published by Scholastic Inc., *Publishers since 1920.* SCHOLASTIC and associated logos are trademarks and/or registered trademarks of Scholastic Inc.

ISBN 978-1-338-74519-1

1 2021

Printed in the U.S.A.   23
First printing 2021
Book design by Baily Crawford

To all the frontline and essential workers—
the real-life heroes. Thank you.

1

It's a Thursday in mid-March. There are teases of spring in the air, and the sun seems to be staying out just a little bit longer each day. Aside from that, though, it's a pretty average, unforgettable Thursday.

I'm walking through the hallway of my high school with Vanessa, my girlfriend. It's just after lunch, and I only have two classes left until my day is done.

Vanessa squeezes my hand. "You're still coming over after school today, right, Claire?" she asks, peering at me with her huge blue eyes.

I squeeze her hand back. "I wouldn't miss it for anything in the world."

She smiles, and even though we've been dating for almost five months, her smile is still so electric, and I can't help but smile back.

"Oh, get a room, you two," someone says behind us.

I whip around, annoyed, ready to scowl at whoever said it, but it's just Gaby. She sits between Vanessa and me in physics class, and she gets stuck in the middle of our whispered conversations all the time.

I stick my tongue out at her, while Vanessa squeezes my hand harder, laughing.

"We have a lot of homework to work on!" Vanessa says.

Gaby rolls her eyes, and I start to say, "I need a lot of help with—"

But then the loudspeaker overhead crackles to life. Everyone in the hall reflexively covers their ears as the speakers squeak and squeal. Principal Shaffier taps the microphone like he always does, the signal for everyone to settle down and uncover their ears.

"Um, good afternoon, students," he says, then pauses. Which is a little weird. Usually his announcements seem like they start when he's in the middle of thinking about something.

There is a whoosh over the speakers, which I realize is him exhaling deeply. Also weird. Vanessa and I look at each other, a glimmer of confusion in her eyes.

Then comes another whoosh, another deep breath, and I look around the hallway. Some students look confused, some look annoyed; some are still chattering away to each other without a care in the world.

"I'm sorry, but I've never had to make an announcement like this before," he finally admits.

"Spit it out!" Simon Jacobson yells. His meathead friends crack up like it's the funniest thing they've ever heard. There are so many of them, and they're all standing way too close to us, laughing so loud I don't catch everything Principal Shaffier says. All I hear is something about "unprecedented times."

"Will you please shut up?!" someone hisses at them.

They act all insulted, muttering to each other. Now I can hear the principal loud and clear.

But I kind of wish they'd be loud and awful again because even though I can hear what the principal is saying now, I don't fully understand it. He's saying something about the virus—this virus that we've all been hearing about for a few weeks. I've heard my parents talking about what was happening in Japan, in Italy—the rising number of infections and lives lost all over the world—but it wasn't supposed to be something that could ever happen in our country, in our lives. That's what they told me, anyway.

But now it's here. It's in New York.

"We've just received word of over fifty cases of the virus in hospitals all over the city, with many more suspected, and many more awaiting positive confirmation," Principal Shaffier says, his voice quivering a little. "Per the governor's emergency state-mandated protocol, our school will be closed for two weeks. We will be switching to remote learning, as we have seen schools in other parts of the world do. Your teachers are working hard to determine what exactly this will entail, so be sure to check your emails. In the meantime, there will be no in-person school tomorrow, in order for your teachers to prepare for the next two weeks."

Simon and his friends start cheering and yelling, "No school tomorrow! Let's party!"

But this time a lot more people are annoyed with them. Even Fred Parris, the obligatory class clown, who seems to pride himself on how bad his grades are, yells, "Shut UP!"

Simon and his friends still look mostly insulted, but one of them, I can't remember his name, says kind of half-heartedly, "Yeah, guys, this sounds important."

Principal Shaffier continues, "I'm going to repeat myself because I know this is a lot to process. We are hopeful that over the next two weeks we can adequately clean and disinfect and install proper filtration devices throughout the school. During that time, you will still be responsible for your assignments and projects just as you are now. It is strongly encouraged that you stay home and isolate in lockdown with your family."

A flurry of whispers erupts around me. Even Simon Jacobson doesn't have a clever joke to make in this moment.

"This is not just an order from me, but from the governor as well," Principal Shaffier goes on. "This is not a snow day; this is not a drill. This is a pandemic, a very serious situation, and I know you will all do what you can to ensure that we can return to school and normal life as quickly as possible."

I look around, but everyone seems as confused as I feel. Vanessa squeezes my hand again, and I realize one of us is shaking.

"Your parents and guardians have been notified via email, text, and phone call about the situation, tomorrow's school closure, and today's early dismissal," Principal Shaffier informs. "Many of them could be receiving similar news from their employers about staying home and working remotely from their offices for the next two weeks as well. Be safe, get home quickly, and we'll see you all in two weeks."

"What early dismissal?" I say to Vanessa. But everyone else around me is talking, and my voice is almost lost in the roar of the crowded hallway, a mix of excitement and confusion. Some students are cheering and laughing, but most look like I feel, as if they're also still processing what they just heard.

Vanessa looks at me, puzzled as well, and says, "Yeah, I guess the day is over now. I'm going to head to my locker. I'll meet you by your locker in a few?"

I nod, but I don't move.

"Hey," Vanessa says, gently tugging on my hand, and I try to snap out of my daze. She does it again, then guides me over to my locker. "I'm going to go pack up whatever I might need for the next . . . gosh, two weeks. I'll come back in a few minutes and we can walk to my place together?"

I look at her, but it's like my mouth has forgotten how to work.

Vanessa gently touches my face, makes my eyes meet hers. "It's going to be okay, Claire. Just get your stuff together, all right?" I must have nodded, because Vanessa looks satisfied. "I'll be right back."

I watch her go, then turn back to my locker and open it. But it's like I've never seen the things inside it before. I stand there, looking at nothing, and I get jostled by two girls. One has her turtleneck sweater pulled up over her mouth and nose. She says something to me, but I can't hear her, and I don't recognize her with half her face covered. Her friend gives me an apologetic look, but they're swept down the hallway with the rest of the crowd.

When Vanessa comes back a few minutes later, I'm still standing in front of my locker, digging through piles of crinkled papers, trying to figure out what I might need for the next two weeks.

"Babe, do you need some help?" she asks, looking at me sympathetically.

I look at her, her wavy brownish-reddish hair in a neat ponytail. Her black flowered dress is clean and unwrinkled, and even her boots are tied perfectly.

She doesn't wait for me to answer and steps forward. She starts pulling textbooks and notebooks out of my locker and putting them in my backpack. I watch her, and then I finally speak. "How are you so calm?"

The hallway is mostly emptied out now, so she actually hears me this time.

She turns to me, zipping up my backpack. "Freaking out won't do anything, ya know?"

I nod. Of course, she's right. She's always right.

She hands me my backpack. "Ready to go?"

I nod again, because it seems like that's all I can do.

Vanessa and I hold hands on the walk to her apartment. She's quieter than usual, and I'm still having trouble speaking. Trouble thinking. Every once in a while, she says something, about how she's glad she cleaned up her bedroom desk last week, how she's glad her desk chair is so comfortable.

But the principal's words are still echoing through my head. *Lockdown, pandemic, isolate.*

The sidewalks are bustling with other students, with other people, and it's almost like a normal day, except that we're out of school two hours early. I keep hearing snatches of conversations. All anyone is talking about is the virus and the lockdown.

"I wish I had gone to the grocery store yesterday," I hear a passerby say. "I definitely don't have enough food to last two weeks."

"Doesn't matter. Shelves are empty," another responds.

"Can't find hand sanitizer anywhere either," someone else chimes in.

My head buzzes, trying to understand everything I'm hearing around me.

When we're almost at Vanessa's apartment building, something occurs to me, and I finally speak. "Wait, Vanessa, if we're supposed to stay home, in quarantine or lockdown or whatever . . . should we be hanging out right now?"

Vanessa smiles, then scrunches up her face as she thinks about it. "I mean, we've already been together at school. What difference will a few more hours make?"

I nod, agreeing with her logic. But something else is bugging me. "What about after today? When can we see each other again?"

"You heard the principal," Vanessa says. "We'll stay home for two weeks. But we can still see each other on video chats. And look at the bright side: I bet this will give you more time to think about the schools you want to apply to!"

"Right. College stuff. Just what I want." I try to keep the sarcasm out of my voice, but I don't think it works, because Vanessa gives me a dirty look.

"And just think," she says, unlocking the door to her building, "two weeks of no school lunches, no rushing to classes, and no dealing with the annoyingness of daily high school life."

That's true. A couple weeks away from school might do me some good. I could finally update my Babble account, this app where people can post book reviews and even share their own original stories with others. I've had it for so long that it still has my original screenname, Clarissareads—a pseudonym my mom came up with when I was younger to protect my identity. I'm actually kind of looking forward to it now.

"I guess you're right," I say.

But Vanessa doesn't hear me. She's looking at something on her phone as we walk up the stairs.

My phone! Suddenly, I realize that I haven't checked it since before Principal Shaffier's announcement. I wonder if my parents have tried to get in touch with me at all. If they'll be working from home too. That would mean all three of us home at the same time, together, for two weeks. Together. In our tiny Brooklyn apartment.

I shake the thought from my head and pull my phone out of my back pocket. Oops. Eleven missed calls, and a bunch of text messages. A whole bunch of text messages. Almost all from my mom, and she's freaking out. Big time.

Uh-oh.

Mom:

> C, I heard your school is getting out early and will be closed tomorrow. I'm heading home now too. When are you getting home?

> I'm home, where are you?

> Why aren't you answering your phone?

> Your dad hasn't heard from you either.

> Claire, pick up your phone!!!

Dad:

> Claire, where are you? Mom is really worried.

> Call your mother.

I'm on the third floor, Vanessa's floor. I don't even remember walking up here.

She's standing in front of the door to her apartment, keys in one hand, reading something on her phone.

"Vanessa, I think I need to—"

"Claire, maybe we shouldn't—"

I take a breath and wait for her to go first.

"Maybe we shouldn't hang out right now," she says quickly. "My parents left work early and are both picking up Lucy from school, and then coming home."

I nod, suddenly feeling like I want to cry. "Yeah, I think my mom is pretty freaked. I should head home."

"I understand."

And then we just look at each other.

"So . . . I'll see you at school in two weeks?" Vanessa finally says.

"Two weeks. That's half a month." My throat hurts from trying to swallow my tears back. "That's a long time."

"Aw, babe," Vanessa says softly. She walks over to where I'm standing and pulls me in for a hug. We're both still wearing our backpacks, so it should be an awkward hug, but it's not. It's comfortable, comforting, the way it always is to touch her, and realizing I can't do it for two weeks makes the tears spill out of my eyes.

Vanessa takes a step back, looks into my face, and gently wipes my tears away with her thumb, then softly kisses my cheeks. She smells like the lavender shampoo she uses . . . and like Vanessa.

Like my girlfriend.

"We can video-chat all the time. Like, do homework together over it. Maybe even watch movies or TV or something?"

She's trying to make me feel better, and she's right—we can still talk, still see each other. But knowing it'll be over a screen, not in person—that I won't be able to smell her lavender shampoo for two weeks—feels just so gut-wrenchingly horrible. I swallow my tears again and nod. I don't trust myself not to cry.

Vanessa leans forward again, kisses my lips softly, then more intensely, and my hands are in her lavender hair, and her hands are in my chin-length bob, until finally she pulls away.

"Okay, okay. It's just two weeks, right?" she says, laughing. "We'll be a few blocks away from each other too. It's not like one of us is going to the moon or anything. And just think how much college stuff you can get figured out!"

"Right," I say weakly. But somewhere deep down, I feel like she might as well be going to the moon.

"I know it's overwhelming, babe. Just try for an hour or two a day, looking places up online, reading student message boards, that kind of thing."

"Right," I say again, even more weakly this time.

We hear the building door open downstairs. "That's probably my family," she says.

"Okay, I should go." I want to say more, so much more, but I don't even know where to begin. I want to ask more, too, but I know she doesn't have any answers. So I just give her another peck on the lips, one more quick hug, and I head down the stairs.

But Vanessa was wrong—it wasn't her parents and Lucy walking into the building. I want to go back upstairs, spend a few more precious seconds with her, but I think of my mom.

Oh god. My mom.

When I get outside, I dig my phone out of my pocket again. More missed calls and texts. I don't read the texts and just call my mom. The phone doesn't even ring.

"Claire! Where are you? Why weren't you answering? Do you have any idea how worried I've been?"

"Mom, I'm sorry. I was at Vanessa's. I'm coming home—"

"Vanessa's? What on earth were you doing at Vanessa's? You were supposed to come straight home! You know we're in a lockdown, right? In a pandemic?"

"I'm sorry!" I say again.

"That's it? You're sorry?"

"Yes, I'm sorry! What else do you want me to say?"

My mom sighs. "I just don't know why you didn't come home right away. I just . . ." And then I realize she's crying.

"Claire, you're coming home, right?" Now it's my dad on the phone.

"Yes, I'm on my way." I don't know why, but I feel really annoyed. And a little dazed. "Why is Mom so freaked out?"

My dad sighs. "Let's talk when you get home, okay, Claire?"

"Fine," I say, and hang up.

I walk the rest of the way quickly, and I hear more snatches of conversations around me:

"My landlord's sister has it."

"I heard it's worse for the elderly."

"I heard it's worse for people with lung problems."

"Can't find toilet paper anywhere!"

I don't understand what toilet paper has to do with this virus, with me not being able to go to school or see my girlfriend for two weeks. But I quickly stop thinking about it, about anything, really, when I see the bodega in my neighborhood. The bodega I've been going to since I was in second grade—that I've bought probably thousands of bags of chips from, that never has more than a handful of people inside at once—has a line of people waiting to go in. A long line. One woman has a scarf wrapped around the bottom part of her face; a man is wearing a pair of goggles. I walk more quickly.

When I turn the corner to my street, I see my mom standing outside our building. She's got her head down, looking at her phone, but then looks up and sees me. She runs down the block with her arms out. People on the sidewalks watch her, watch me, and I even see one person take out their phone. To take a video? Call the police? I don't have time to see, because suddenly I'm wrapped in her arms so tight I can barely breathe.

"Claire, I was so worried," my mom says into my hair.

"It's okay, Mom," I gasp.

She loosens her grip, pulls back to look at my face. Her eyes are red, and her face is splotchy, like she's been crying. I've never seen her look so scared and sad at the same time.

She wraps an arm around my shoulder. "Let's get inside."

Inside. Where I'll spend the next two weeks.

We walk up to the second floor, to our apartment, and I almost trip over the grocery bags lining the hallway inside.

"What is all this stuff?" I ask.

My dad emerges from the kitchen. "All this should hopefully last two weeks. Mom and I started stocking up on things here and there at our offices, and we brought it home today."

"Oh god, my office," my mom says, and she looks like she's about to cry again.

"Soooo, you guys will be working at home for the next two weeks?" I ask quietly, still trying to understand what's happening. "I just . . . I thought you said this wouldn't happen here?"

My thinking out loud seems to make my mom feel worse, and I see her lip trembling.

"Yep! We're going to be spending a lot of quality family time together," my dad says brightly. He comes over to wrap his arms around me, but I shrug him off, nodding my head at my mom.

"Oh, Mom is just upset, trying to figure out how this is all going to work. You know, working at home. All of us together."

My mom looks at him, sniffling. "Do you seriously think that's all I'm worried about? Do you even know anything about me, Joe? I'm worried about the fact that there is a rapidly spreading virus out there. That we don't know how many people are going to get sick. How many are going to die. That I didn't know where my only daughter—my only child—was until about five minutes ago."

My dad grins. "I think it was more like nine minutes."

"Dad!"

"Joe!"

My mom stomps down the hall to the bathroom. The water to the shower turns on, which we both know she does when she wants to cry. Loud.

"Good one, Dad," I say. But I'm also replaying her words in my head. *Rapidly spreading virus. Sick. Die.* And I'm replaying how scared and sad she was. How scared and sad she *is*. How even if my parents said this virus wouldn't come here, it did. How it's here. How little they might actually know about this virus. How little *anyone* might actually know about this virus.

"What?" he says, still with the silly grin on his face.

"You're unreal," I say, and then go to my room and slam the door.

2

Posted by Clarissareads:

Well, here we are, a month into lockdown.

I know Babble is mostly supposed to be for book reviews and fan fiction, but I'm caught up on my reviews, and I feel like I want to write something. Anything. Maybe someday I'll want to look back on this time. I can't imagine why, but, here I am. Where I always am. Right here. A month into lockdown. It was supposed to be two weeks, and then it was supposed to be two weeks, and then spring break got moved up (not much of a "break," though, since we couldn't go anywhere), and then one week got added after that.

It's the middle of April now, and we're supposed to go back to school the first week of May. I've actually missed school, how weird is that? I miss how gross the cafeteria smells on chili days; I miss wondering which way the principal will have his hair combed over; I miss the sound of the crowded hallways; I miss sitting at a school desk and changing desks and rooms between classes; I miss seeing people other than my parents. I reallllly miss people in general.

The first week of lockdown actually wasn't so bad. It

was just kind of like a long snow day. Lots of snacks, movies, pajamas, reading; lots of time on Babble, writing reviews, reading all your great stories; lots of video chats. But now, a month into this whole thing, the novelty of lockdown is starting to wear off. I can't believe I'm actually saying this, but I'm starting to get a little tired of yoga pants.

And it's been getting harder and harder to ignore the news, which my parents always seem to have on. I can't wrap my head around how many people have gotten sick, how many have died. How many people have lost their jobs. How many people's lives have changed forever.

So I don't let myself. It's too much.

One sorta good thing I've picked up from the constant news is that the number of people testing positive is going down in the city. That this lockdown thing is working. I mean, it better be. Anyone who wants to enter New York has to quarantine for fourteen days. We're not allowed out of New York unless it's for "essential" business. I sit on my fire escape to read sometimes, but aside from that, I only go out of my apartment every few days, for quick morning strolls around the block with my mom. We never see many people, but it still feels dangerous somehow, like we're doing something we aren't supposed to, even with our medical masks on and keeping our distance from the few people we see.

So that's something, at least. Lockdown works. Masks work. Social distancing works. It's just too bad it couldn't have been something for all the thousands of people who have already died. For their families. And it's too bad more places around the country aren't doing it, because cases are going up everywhere else.

Oh, another bad thing I've picked up, not from the news but from the living room: My mom might get laid off. She works as a graphic designer for a travel agency, and surprise, surprise, demand for travel isn't very high during a pandemic. I'm not even supposed to know that, but turns out it's hard to keep secrets when you're in lockdown in an apartment. My parents keep telling me not to worry, that everything will be okay. But they also told me not to worry about the virus, that it wouldn't happen here.

Look how that turned out.

Likes: 3

Comments: 0

3

I watch Vanessa as she bends her head down over her math homework. She's wrestling a precalculus equation, and I'm trying to come up with a good thesis statement for my English essay on *The Book Thief.* Vanessa whispers to herself as she calculates, erases, calculates again, and erases some more. She sighs, puts down her pencil, and rubs her neck. I reach out my hand instinctively to massage where she is rubbing, but my hand bonks against my laptop screen.

Vanessa looks up at me, startled.

"Sorry," I say.

"It's okay. What was that?"

"Oh, it was my hand." I shrug. "Old habits die hard or something."

"No, not that. I heard a text. Like, maybe a few texts?"

And then I hear it too—the ping of text messages hitting our laptops. It's not a sound either of us is unfamiliar with, but the pings keep coming, until it's a hailstorm of incoming texts.

"I'll see what's going on," Vanessa says. "Want to check yours, too, Claire?"

"Oh, right," I say. Vanessa is perpetually a step ahead of me in everything. I click over and see that I have ten new messages. Weird.

"Oh, wow," she says, a hint of disbelief in her voice. "No in-person school for the rest of the year."

"What? How could that be?" I read the message from the school, but it doesn't make sense. "I thought we were supposed to go back the first week of May? Next week?" My palms are starting to sweat, and I'm getting a tingly feeling in my fingers. I take some deep breaths. "Vanessa, what's happening?" I ask, unable to hide the shaking in my voice. "When will I be able to see you in person again? It's already been so long."

But Vanessa doesn't answer me. She's reading the texts, eyes moving back and forth. I try to steady my breathing, to control my sweaty, tingly hands.

"Babe, are you reading all these messages and emails?" she asks. I can tell by where her eyes are that she's still reading, not looking at my face.

"Um, I just read the one from school." Not that I processed or retained anything that it said. Vanessa doesn't seem to notice the shaking in my voice.

"Yeah, well, there are some others. From the superintendent. Oh, my parents . . ." I can hear her typing.

"Wait, who are you texting?" I ask shrilly.

"I was just writing my mom back. Silly, since she's in the next room, but I bet she's in a meeting or something." And then she laughs. She actually laughs.

"This isn't good, Vanessa!" I yell. "When can we see each other again?"

Vanessa finally looks at me and furrows her eyebrows. "I need to turn your volume down a bit," she says, tapping at her keyboard.

"Aren't you freaking out?" I ask, clearly freaking out myself. "I mean, this must mean the virus is really bad. We were supposed to go back next week! I'm scared. I don't want anyone else to get sick. And I miss you! I just want to give you a hug so bad. Like, when can that even happen again?"

She looks at me calmly over the screen. "I miss you, too, Claire. But, I mean, none of this is really that big of a surprise, is it?"

"It isn't?" I say weakly.

"Babe, haven't you been following the news? Schools have been closed for the rest of the year all over the country. We knew this was a possibility."

"We did? Why didn't you tell me that?"

"Um, because I didn't think it was my responsibility? And I figured you were reading and watching the news?"

"I am," I say defensively. "I just . . . I guess I didn't think it would really happen." I bite my lip to fight back my tears. "This is awful! And I . . . I just want to see you."

"I wish I could see you too," Vanessa says, still just as calmly as before. "But staying home, staying apart, is what we need to do right now. Sending us all back to school would just make the cases go up like crazy. Especially since they're so high everywhere else. And we have everything we need at our fingertips. Between my laptop, my phone, my tablet, my watch, I'm always connected to someone, somewhere. So . . . I guess what I'm saying is that we should be thankful."

"Thankful?"

"Of course," she says slowly. "Plus, most important of all, we're healthy. And young. It's going to be okay. Stop freaking out, babe."

"That seems easier said than done."

I don't think Vanessa hears what I just said. I can tell by her eyes that she's looking at something else on her screen, and then I hear her fingers typing again. The panic I was feeling before is starting to become anger. But I'm not totally sure who it's directed at, or why.

I stare at her, not sure what I'm supposed to do, to say, trying to calm the panicked anger I feel, when she finally looks at me again. "Well, I should go talk to my mom and dad. And Lucy. My parents keep texting me, and obviously we're all in the same apartment!"

"Okay," I say.

She looks like she's expecting me to say more, so I say, "I should do that too. Talk to my family." When in doubt, I've always followed Vanessa's lead. Why stop now?

"Cool, talk soon." She looks at me for a second and says, "I love you, Claire. It's going to be okay." Then she blows me a kiss and ends the call.

I walk out into the living room, expecting it to look different somehow, like I've entered another dimension, the dimension of no school for the rest of the year. But it looks pretty much the same as it did when I came out for lunch a few hours ago. My mom is on the couch, working on her laptop, and my dad is probably in their room, working on his own.

The TV is actually off, and it's mercifully quiet.

"Hey, honey," my mom says as I walk in. She looks way too calm to have heard about my school closing.

She goes back to her computer, tapping at the keys, sighing at her work, and I want her to have this moment, not the next moment when I tell her I won't be going to school for the rest of the year. And then it dawns on me: If schools are closed, she and Dad might not be going back to their offices either. And this definitely won't be good news for my mom's job. I watch her working until she looks up at me.

"Sorry, do you need a snack?" she asks. "There's fruit in the fridge, pretzels in the pantry. Which reminds me—I need to get started on our next grocery delivery order . . ."

"Mom, I don't need a snack. I'm not eight."

"Right, sorry," she says, laughing. This lockdown has been the longest stretch of time our family has spent just the three of us since my dad's paternity leave with me. Sometimes I think we all forget that I'm seventeen, and what stage of life we're all in.

"You okay?" she says, looking at me more closely.

"Mom, there's no more in-person school. Like, until fall. And I wouldn't be surprised if you didn't go back to work either. And like your job . . ."

She looks at me, confused.

"Don't you get texts on your computer? Where is your phone? Wasn't there a work email? Turn on the news! Check something!" I say, my panicked anger returning.

"Claire, take a deep breath." She clicks some things on her laptop. "I'm trying to keep my phone put away while I work, and I had to take texts off my computer. I don't know how you get anything done with those constant alerts coming in from every direction! I must have disabled the alerts on my work email accidentally."

While she's clicking, the door to my parents' bedroom opens, and my dad comes out, smiling. "Looks like someone is starting summer vacation early!"

"What?" my mom and I snap at the same time.

"The governor's orders?" my dad says. "Jeez, don't you guys check the news, or at least social media? This is kind of a thing."

He goes to the kitchen and opens the fridge while I watch my mom read her email. "Oh my god," she says quietly.

My dad emerges from the fridge, holding a container of yogurt. "Honey, do we have a grocery order coming anytime soon?"

My mom is still reading email and doesn't answer.

"Melissa? Did you hear me?"

My mom finally looks up, distracted. "What? Did you say something, Joe?"

"Yeah, I wanted to know if we had a grocery order coming soon," he says as he digs a spoon out of the drawer.

"I don't know, do we?" my mom says. "I told you before, I'm not the only one in charge of the grocery orders. It's your responsibility too."

"Okay, okay." My dad spoons yogurt into his mouth. "Valid point. I'll definitely add more of this to our cart. Cake-flavored yogurt might be one of the best food inventions ever."

My mom and I are both watching him, frowning.

"What?" he says, his mouth full.

"God, Dad, how are you thinking about yogurt at a time like this?"

"She's right," my mom adds, crossing her arms. "Also, that stuff is loaded with sugar. You might as well eat a candy bar."

"Great! I'll add candy bars to our grocery cart online too," my dad says, pulling his phone out of his pocket.

"What is *wrong* with you?" I snap.

"Nothing is wrong with me. I've been in lockdown for a month, remember?" my dad says, winking.

"I can't deal with him," I say, looking at my mom.

"Joe, take it down a notch, okay? It's not the time. Did you forget the part about our daughter not being able to go to school for the rest of the year? My company is working from home through the summer. What about yours? This is really, really scary." My mom stands up and paces.

"Yes, of course," my dad says, shrugging. "Got the email from my company while I was reading about New York schools. I mean, are you guys really surprised by this? Does anyone watch the news around here besides me?"

"You sound like Vanessa," I say.

My dad bows. "I will take that as a compliment."

I roll my eyes.

"Just because we knew it was a possibility doesn't discount that this is still a shock for all of us. We were told two weeks, then two more weeks, and now we're looking at months. Seasons passing, changing. A big chunk of our only child's high school experience. Time when she's supposed to focus on her studies, think about college. This is a lot to take in," my mom says, breathing big, deep breaths.

"You knew it was a possibility too?" I say, turning to face my mom. I feel annoyed at yet another mention of college.

"Yes, honey. It's not like any of this information was hidden from you, though. A total school-year closure was mentioned in the emails and texts that went out to students and parents. It's been on the news. This definitely isn't going to help the 'possible temporary reduction in workforce' thing at my job either."

She says the last part distractedly. She's got her eyes closed, and I can tell she's trying to calm her breathing.

"Is your job going to be okay, Mom?" I ask. "I can't believe any of this."

"Yes, honey, don't worry!" she says quickly, opening her eyes to look at me, and I see tears start to well up in her eyes. "I know high school can be a drag, but you still deserve to finish out your junior year in person. Deserve to see your friends, your girlfriend, in person. I just . . . hate this for you."

Oh god, whenever my mom starts to cry about something related to me, I start to cry, so I quickly wave my hand, like I'm trying to fan the tears dry in my eyes, then give her a hug. "Thanks, Mom."

"Looks like we're about to have a whole lot more family time!" my dad says, rinsing out his empty yogurt container. He has a rainbow-colored yogurt blob stuck to his beard.

"Oh god," my mom and I say at the same time.

Then we all laugh nervously, and I go to my room to cry.

I toss and turn all night. Every time I wake up, I check my phone, read news about the virus, about its spread, about school closures not just in New York, but other states too. I read about the people dying from the virus. All over the world, all over our country, all over our state, and all over our city. I find an online message board for our neighborhood, and I read about the virus here. I find out the old man who lives five blocks over, who feeds the neighborhood stray cats, died last week. I read about food shortages everywhere, lines to get in grocery stores, people being fired from their jobs, companies going out of business.

Finally, I give up doomscrolling and open Babble. I reread my latest post, about my time in lockdown so far. Three likes. No comments. Typical. Maybe I should just write another review. I try to start one about the latest David Levithan book, but all I write is, "I love this book." But then I scroll through my other reviews and realize almost all of them start this way. Sigh.

I poke around Babble a little more, read some reviews of young adult books, read posts about how other people are spending time during the pandemic. I even read a short story someone wrote about life in lockdown. It's a good distraction for a bit, and I decide maybe I should try writing something else that isn't a review. But what?

Thankfully, Babble has a writing prompts section to help users get going. *Write about the best day of your life. Write about the worst day of your life. Write about your favorite childhood toy. Write about what you see right now.* I look around my room, the room I'm starting to get tired of a month into lockdown. My creative writing teacher freshman year told us to write what we know. I sure know my bedroom, the view from my bedroom, pretty well these days. I get out of bed, pull open my gray curtain, and lift open my window. Then I sit at my desk, turn on my laptop, and start writing.

4

My curtain is gray. It matches the blue-gray flowers on my yellow duvet cover. Gray. Were designers foretelling the future when they decided gray would be the new "it" color? So silly that anyone, myself included, ever cared about things like colors matching. That I used to waste time on things like deciding how patterns and colors should come together, in my room or on my body.

I look past my gray curtain to the matching gray sky. I realize the sun hasn't come out in three days. I now feel too familiar with its habits. And lately its habit has been hiding. Not that I blame it. Everyone has been inside, bathing themselves in artificial light, in the glow of their computer screens, their phones, their TVs. Maybe the sun is on strike. Maybe it'll stay on strike the rest of the spring and summer.

I let my eyes make a slow loop from the gray sky down to the apartment building across the street from mine, about fifty feet away. It's a three-story, three-family redbrick, just like mine, and it's bathed in a grayish light, just like I'm sure my building is, too, like everything is.

But this time the receptors in my brain pick up on

something different about the building across the street than usual. Sitting on the fire escape is a teenage girl who looks like she's probably about my age. But I don't recognize her. I've never seen her before. Not on the fire escape, not coming or going from that building, not even at school. Weird. Her head is down, looking at a book in her lap, so I can't really see her face. Her hair is this dark chocolate color. I wonder what her hair would look like on a sunny day, if it would glow. Her hair sweeps in front of her eyes, and as I'm looking at her, she lifts her head, and I notice her head is shaved on one side.

Now she's looking right at me. She's too far away for me to see what color her eyes are, but not far away enough to see that she's not smiling at me. I try smiling at her, but it's been a while since the muscles in my face have shown happiness, and it kind of hurts. The girl looks a little confused. She lifts her hand, and I figure she's going to turn a page in her book, but then she waves her fingers.

At me.

I wonder if she can see the blush spreading across my face—across my body—from where she is. But as I'm deciding if I should wave back, she picks up her book, crawls back into her window, and closes it behind her. She leans on the ledge, looking down at our street, and I wait for her to lift her head again, to give any indication that she actually saw me, that I didn't just imagine whatever exchange it was we had, but all she does is close her curtain, disappearing as quickly as she appeared.

I keep looking outside my window, waiting for the curtain to move again in what I guess to be her room, but the curtain is motionless.

My first time in a month having a social exchange with someone besides my family, not on a laptop or phone screen, and I've already messed it up. Typical. I don't know why, but I feel tears well up in my eyes. I shouldn't be surprised that I've messed up such a basic interaction—one of the things I'm best at is how bad I am at talking to people, after all.

I try not to blink too hard, because I know if I do, the tears will come spilling out.

Likes: 9

Comments: 1

5

I pull my attention away from Babble, distracted by the pinging sound of a text.

Vanessa:

Good morning!

 I wipe my eyes, try to concentrate on my texts with her, and not on what just happened with the girl across the street.

 Or what didn't happen, actually. Seventeen years on this planet and I still don't know how to interact with strangers.

 Vanessa and I text for a bit, until I realize I'm staring off into space, looking out my window again.

 Vanessa asks if I'm there.

 There. Where else can I go but there? But here.

Claire:

Yes, sorry, talking to my mom.

Vanessa:

Hi, Mrs. Draper!

Claire:

She says hi too.

I look around my empty room. A white lie never killed anyone, right?

I tell her I'll talk to her soon, and then I grab some cereal from the kitchen.

I go back to my room and sit at my desk again. I drum my fingers, and my hand wanders past my bowl of cereal, over to my sketch-book, and then to one of my pencils. I open up the sketchbook, find a blank page, and start drawing. I draw a girl. I'm not sure who she is yet. Her eyes are closed, her head is down. But as I draw, I just feel like I want to cry. Maybe scream. Maybe both at the same time. Usually when I draw, I feel recharged, energized, but working on this sketch just makes me feel even worse.

I sigh and put my pencil down. Then I turn to a new blank page, and before I know what I'm doing, I draw the fire escape across the street, the girl I saw. Except in my drawing, she's smiling. I try to draw myself, too, but I can never get my face right. Especially now. I have no idea how to draw a smile anymore.

Suddenly, I smell something burning.

I'm not sure what it is because, well, it's burning, and I'm also still not used to the smell of cooking food in my apartment, even after all the home-cooked meals the last month. I'm still used to the smell of delivered food, food from a whole lot of countries I've never been to. Different food from a different country for each day of the week.

I head out of my room, down the hall, and the smell gets stronger. As I walk into the kitchen, my mom leans over the oven with an oven mitt on, then yanks out a smoking pan. As if on cue, the fire alarm goes off. She slams the smoking pan down on the top of the stove, next to a bubbling pot, then runs over to the smoke detector, waving her mitt in front of it to try to make it stop. My dad emerges from their bedroom, holding his laptop. He's shouting something, but it's too hard to hear what it is over the blaring smoke alarm.

As my mom waves her mitt, the pot on the stove starts to spill over. My dad is still shouting, holding his laptop, so I grab a towel and pick the bubbling pot off the burner. The alarm stops, and we can all hear my dad shouting, "What is going on out here?"

My mom turns around and wipes sweaty hair off her face. "I'm cooking."

"Is that what this is called?" my dad says, but he's smiling.

"I found a recipe on Pinterest for these sweet potato fries. I don't know what I did wrong; I followed the directions exactly."

"And what about this?" I ask, holding the bubbling pot.

Both my mom and dad turn to face me. My mom smacks herself on the forehead. "The quinoa!"

"I'm sure it'll all be delicious, dear," my dad says, his eyes already on his laptop screen again as he heads back to their room. "Can't be any worse than this former vegan's attempt to make bacon the other day."

"Oh, I didn't know you were vegan, Dad," I say.

He looks up, surprised. "Really? Oh, in that case, I was vegan for—"

"Five years, Dad. Yes, you mention it just about every day. I was kidding."

He scowls. "I don't bring it up every day."

"Fine, every other day," I say.

My mom chuckles. "Nice one, Claire." Then she waves the oven mitt at him and says, "Can't wait to see what you come up with for dinner!"

My dad scowls at both of us this time, and he closes the door to their room.

My mom faces me again. "He makes it too easy sometimes. Anyway! Would you rather have cereal or frozen pizza for lunch?"

I look at the pot in my hand and the charred sweet potatoes on the baking sheet. "Something can be salvaged, right?" I try.

"Doubtful." My mom wipes her sweaty hair off her head again. "Unless you like your sweet potatoes with a side of fire."

I peer over her shoulder, study the charred specimen. "I think you mean ash with a side of fire, Mom."

My mom laughs, then gets that look on her face that means she's about to cry. "Don't, Mom," I say quickly.

She turns her head away from me and waves her hand. "I'm sorry! I told myself I wouldn't cry today. I made it all the way until almost lunchtime! I just . . . hate this. All of this. Five months before you set foot inside your school again. We're still figuring out the details with work, but it'll probably be the same for your dad and me, working from home, and stuff is kind of up in the air with me for work . . . I just hate this. And I'm a terrible cook."

"I know, Mom. I hate it too."

She turns to me, her face a little splotchy, but no tears visible. "And?"

"And what?"

"Aren't you going to say I'm not a terrible cook too?"

My mom and I study each other's faces.

"Don't push it," I say, and we both laugh. "Maybe we should give ourselves a little break with the food stuff? Not every meal has to be, like, Instagram worthy."

"You know, I think you're right," she says. "From now on, we're keeping the food simple. No more Pinterest!" She grabs a spatula, waves it in the air.

"So, um, whatcha thinking?" I ask cautiously.

She's got her back to me, digging around in the fridge. She emerges with a loaf of bread, butter, and cheese. "Grilled cheese."

She turns on the stove top, and I wait for her to say more. "Grilled cheese with caramelized onions? Grilled vegan cheese? Grilled cheese with kale pesto?"

She laughs. "Nope! Just plain old regular grilled cheese. With presliced cheese and everything. Did you know I used to make this for lunch for you every single day when you were three? It was right before I went back to work, and I was just starting to freelance again. You were going to preschool in the mornings. You asked for grilled cheese every single day, and maybe it was the guilt, but I gave it to you every single day."

I don't remember it, and I don't remember anything about preschool, no matter how many pictures she or my dad have shown me of it, but I say, "Oh yeah, I kinda remember that."

"Worked my butt off to get that job, and now"—she flips the sandwich onto a plate, then cuts it diagonally with her spatula—"lunch is served," she says.

I bite into it carefully, and it's actually really good. "Mom, this is awesome," I say between gooey bites.

My mom smiles—like, actually smiles. "Good," she says, patting my hand. Then she makes one for my dad, and one for herself.

After lunch, I head back to my room. I sit at my creaky desk. My parents found it on a Brooklyn sidewalk years before I was born. I get splinters from it sometimes, and the one drawer it has sticks all the time, but I love the desk and wouldn't trade it for anything.

I look across the street at the fire escape, but it remains empty. I look at the curtain that the girl closed, but it remains shut.

I open my laptop, scroll through texts from my friends, from Vanessa. It's amazing how much they all manage to say, how much they put in those text boxes, when so little is happening, so little is changing. Everything is so much the same. Everything will be so much the same for the next five months.

Vanessa sends me a link to a crepe cake she and her sister and their mom are baking now. Vanessa's mom has a full-time office job, just like my mom, and she's in and out of virtual meetings, working on projects, all day, even on weekends, just like my mom, so I don't know how she has the time to find a recipe for crepe cake, let alone make one. Vanessa's mom is even a step ahead of my mom. It must run in the family.

I tell her the cake looks like it'll be yummy, and then I click over to Babble. I don't know what I expect to see—I only have the three followers, and there's a chance one of them is a bot, and no one ever comments on anything I post. Unless it's the possible bot, who always says, *This review is the best.* But I scroll down to the bottom of my post and see *Comments: 1.* Weird. It must be the bot again. I click on the comment, and it takes my brain a few reads before I process the words, but then I finally see *Hey, chin up! Give it another shot. Maybe try saying hi next time. You don't have anything to lose, right? And make sure you write about what happens next!*

What? This must be some kind of joke. Probably a cruel one. No one ever comments on my stuff. I don't recognize the username.

I read the words again.

But what if it's not a joke? What if this person is being genuine?

A text pings into my computer, and I jump. It's from Vanessa, a picture of the crepe cake. I try to focus on the cake, squash down the weird, sort of excited feeling in my chest.

Claire:

Wow, looks amazing!

Vanessa:

How's that college research going? That was your plan for the afternoon, right? Remember, just an hour or two a day! ☺

I sigh, then open up Babble again.

6

It's the weekend. Not that weekends have much significance anymore. It's nice to have a break in online lessons, though. From teachers reminding us to mute our microphones or unmute our microphones. From us reminding our teachers to unmute their microphones.

I wish I could mute thinking about college. Could mute this stupid virus. This lockdown.

But, alas, homework is still here. That part hasn't changed. I do a little bit, slowly texting here and there. As much as I hate to admit it, I've settled into a routine, into a new normal, in this world, this reality that is completely unreal.

I'm doing my homework at my desk, and I open my curtain, then open my window to get in some fresh air. Since it's the weekend, the delivery trucks that usually favor our street aren't driving by, so it's almost kind of quiet out there. Except for the honking. And music in cars. Where is everyone going?

I look across the street ... and the girl is on the fire escape again, book in her lap.

So I didn't imagine her.

She's reading. The sun is actually making a guest appearance today, and the girl is sitting in a little patch of sunlight. Her hair looks like it's glowing. I wondered what it would look like in the sun before, and it does, it actually glows. She slowly runs a hand through her hair. I force myself to tear my eyes away from her, and to focus on my homework, but my eyes keep wandering. The girl is wearing black cutoff jean shorts, a black hoodie, and I wonder if she's warm in the late-spring sun. I try to see what book she's reading, but she's too far away for me to see the cover. All I can tell is that it's a thick book with yellowed pages.

I do some more work, then look up at the girl again. And I wonder, again, how I've never seen her before at school. I mean, it's a huge high school. But I feel like I'd remember seeing her? Maybe she goes to the arts high school, or maybe the private high school. Then I look at her more closely. Or maybe she's older than I thought? That must be it. I tear my eyes away from her and look back at my homework. When I look up again across the street, the girl is gone.

I didn't say hi again, but it's okay. I'm going to keep my chin up.

Likes: 12

Comments: 1

7

The rest of my day and the rest of my homework are uneventful, and I
don't see the girl on the fire escape again. My dad makes boxed pasta for
dinner, with jarred tomato sauce. We all swear not to tell Grandma and
Grandpa that we ate sauce that wasn't homemade. My dad's parents
were born in Italy; they came to the States right before they had my dad,
and my grandmother is an epic cook. My dad is not. But there are no
fire alarms going off, and Pinterest isn't involved. It's one of the best
meals we've had since lockdown started.

After dinner, Vanessa texts me to ask what I want to watch tonight.

I put my phone down, cringing as I think about this new date-
night tradition. Part of the fun of watching movies or TV with Vanessa
before was sitting next to her, holding her hand, feeling the warmth of
her body next to mine. Our first date was at a movie theater in Cobble
Hill. They had cheap matinee prices during the week, and we shared a
bucket of stale popcorn, our fingers bumping together as we watched
Star Wars.

Now? Propping my phone up next to my laptop with both of us on
video calls on our phones? It's just not the same.

Like, I want to watch TV, or a movie, but I want to watch it alone. Truly alone.

But it's cool that she wants to spend so much time with me. And, like, completely flattering. Though, well, I don't totally understand why. Just like I don't totally understand what she sees in me as a girlfriend. She's . . . perfect. Smart, pretty, nice. She does really well in her classes at school, and she's one of those people who can really just get along with anyone. And she's got this wavy brownish-reddish shoulder-length hair that people pay a lot of money for, but hers has just always been that way. And she's confident about her looks, but not conceited. And her eyes. Her eyes! I've heard of different kinds of blue before, like sky blue, or blue like some kind of body of water, but her eyes are bluer than blue. They remind me of the card my mom made for me for Valentine's Day, telling me she loves me bluer than a blueberry.

But as much as I love my smart, pretty, nice girlfriend, I really thought I'd have a lot more alone time in lockdown. We had three classes together at school and the same lunch period, so we used to see each other a lot during the day, talk a lot during the day. That's how we started dating. We saw each other all the time, and then one day in the lunch line we somehow started talking about which movie theaters the subway was loudest in. Like, which actual theater room in each actual cinema across the city. She said theater number six in the Times Square movie theater, and I said it was way louder at the theater in Cobble Hill. I just couldn't remember which actual theater number, and I said that I would go to the movies to check it out soon, and then she said, "Let's go together." And we did. And we saw *Star Wars: The Force Awakens,* the subway rumbling under our feet, even though neither of us had seen any of the other *Star Wars* movies and we didn't really know what was going on.

And then, the relationship just kind of happened. Easily. Comfortably. We'd usually hang out after school, too, doing homework . . . and other things.

But then we'd say good-bye, go home. This watching TV and movies together over video calls thing is new. And kind of exhausting.

But she's my girlfriend. My smart, pretty, nice girlfriend. We've been dating for almost six months. One month of that in a pandemic. I can't see her in person, haven't seen her in person in a month. I should be excited to see her face over a screen, to spend time with her. I'm just being weird.

Claire:

Up to you, babe!

Vanessa:

How about more British Bake Off? I have sweets on my brain after the crepe cake. ☺

Claire:

Sounds good.

I attempt to focus on my imminent chat with my girlfriend. I open up the video-streaming site on my computer, then plug in my laptop to its charger. I'm ready. And at 7:30, right on time, Vanessa starts the video chat with me.

I answer the call. It's so good to see her smiling face. To know that I'm making her smile. Her curly hair is in two loose braids, and it's adorable.

"I have popcorn!" she says, holding up a bowl.

I smile. "Of course you do."

"My mom and Lucy and I found this recipe for kettle corn. I wish you could be here to try it. It took a few tries before we got it right, but it turned out so good!" She pops some into her mouth.

"I wish I could be there too," I say.

"Did you make a snack?" she asks, looking at the bottom of her screen.

"No, not quite," I say. "The day kind of got away from me."

She looks disappointed for a second and then says, "Oh, I hope that means you got lots of college research done!"

"Um, something like that."

She looks at me, frowning.

I haven't told her anything about the possible weirdness with my mom's job, about what it could mean for money for college, because talking about it would make it real, and it all just makes me so tired, so I still don't say anything.

"Anyway!" I say, trying to change the subject. Though I don't know what I'm changing the subject to.

Vanessa does it for me. Picks up the slack for me. "Ready?" she says, sighing. She shows her laptop, with the show queued up on her computer.

We pop in our earbuds, say, "One, two, three," and start the show, with our phones propped up right next to our laptops.

My TV show with Vanessa is, well, sweet. Like, in every sense. She tells me all the steps involved in making the crepe cake and the kettle corn that she and Lucy and their mom made, and I don't mind that she talks over what the judges say about the contestants' show-stoppers. It's cute how excited she gets about baking. How excited she gets about everything. She tells me that they're going to make a treacle tart next, and I remind myself to google that later. There's a chance it was baked on the episode we just watched, but I don't want Vanessa to know I wasn't paying attention to what the contestants were making, even if it was because she was talking to me.

When the show ends, I say good night to her. I take out my earbuds, put my phone and laptop down on my bed, where I've been laying. It's just after ten, and I should be tired. Maybe it's watching all the desserts being baked, thinking about all the sugar, but I feel wide awake. Wired.

I pace around my room, then, mid-pace, open Babble on my phone. I'm just checking to see if anyone said anything about the latest addition to my story. Not that it matters. Not that I care.

The app loads, and *Comments: 1* is under my last post.

Sounds like a step in the right direction! Try, try, try again. And keep writing! You have a way with words.

A way with words. My creative writing teacher told me I was a good writer. I wanted to take more writing classes, and I even thought about signing up for one this spring, but Vanessa reminded me that I should take as many honors and AP classes as I can, for college applications. So I didn't.

I feel my ears burning.

I shake my head. This person is just being nice. But why? Why would someone go out of their way to read my Babble story posts and comment on them? Maybe they think I'm a decent writer? Maybe they are interested in what happens with this girl across the street? I look at my curtain. I wonder if the girl is out there again.

Well, I'm not opening the curtain. Because what if I do, and the girl is on the fire escape again and I do something silly again? What if I forget how to wave, how to speak, again?

Or what if I open it and she's not out there? What if I just imagined the whole thing, her whole existence?

I can't decide which option seems worse.

I reread the comment. They think I have a way with words.

I pace my room, then turn off my light. Before I can stop myself, I take two quick strides over to my window and pull the curtain open.

Then I open my laptop.

8

She's on her fire escape. The light from a streetlamp casts a warm glow all around her. Why is my heart racing? Why are my palms sweating?

I pull my curtain closed just as quickly as I opened it.

I stand there, staring at the curtain again, wondering if maybe I just hallucinated seeing her. Maybe it was just a shadow. Maybe it wasn't actually her. The building is a three-family home, like ours, and it's a couple, like my parents' age, who live there. I've never seen any indication they have a daughter, this daughter. Is this girl all just a product of my imagination? My friends have told me about news reports, stories on the news, about the mental impact the pandemic can have on people. Maybe that's what's happening to me.

I take a deep breath, stare at my curtain, tell myself I'm just trying to prove my mental stability, and I open the curtain, wider this time, at least four inches.

She's still there.

This time I keep the curtain open, watching her, making sure she doesn't turn into smoke and disappear. Before I can stop myself, I open my window and crawl out onto my fire escape, which is right outside my bedroom window.

She doesn't even notice, though, and keeps her head bent over her book. It looks like the same tattered book that she had earlier. She runs her hands through her hair as she reads. It's amazing how still she sits. She doesn't check her phone, her watch, anything. She just . . . reads.

Watching her is really soothing. I'd never guess we were in the middle of a pandemic with how peacefully she sits on the fire escape. After less than a minute of me watching her, she puts the book down and stretches her arms over her head. I need to say something, alert her to my presence; I realize she could look over and see me on my fire escape, but I'm mesmerized watching her.

She puts her arms back down in her lap, then stretches her legs out in front of her, bending over her stretched-out legs.

I'm trying to make my mouth work, and I'm also admiring her flexibility, wondering if she's always been that flexible or if that's something she has trained herself to do, when she suddenly looks up. Right at me. Again.

I should wave, should speak, should do anything besides what I'm doing, which is nothing, but I'm paralyzed again.

She quickly pulls her legs in, grabs her book, and stands up. She cups her hands over her eyes, I think to cut out the glare from the streetlamp. She stands there, staring across the street at me on my fire escape. I think I've forgotten how to breathe. It's like time has slowed down, or like I'm moving underwater, tangled up in seaweed, and any action I want my body to make is going to take too long.

I wait for her to yell something mean, or to ask me what my problem is and why I keep staring at her, why I'm sitting on my fire escape, but she doesn't. She just stands there, like she's stuck in whatever weird time wormhole I'm stuck in, or she's swimming through the same seaweedy water as me.

And then her body moves again, and she waves. And, strangest of all, she's smiling at me. Then, as I'm trying to process what's happening, what just happened, she grabs her book, and climbs back inside, shuts her window, and closes her curtain. I'm left wondering once again, was it all a dream?

Likes: 36

Comments: 5

9

That night my sleep is full of dreams about me trying to catch up with someone on the sidewalk outside my apartment, reaching for someone whose face I can't see, whose hand keeps slipping from my grasp every time I make a grab for it.

The dreams seem endless, and apparently they are, because when I wake up and check my phone, I see that it's almost 11:00 a.m.

Oh well. It's still the weekend. And not like I have anywhere to go, anywhere to be. Not like I ever have anywhere to go, anywhere to be, no matter the day of the week.

I stretch in bed and scroll through my phone. Some texts from Vanessa, wishing me good morning, asking what I'm doing today, and then, finally, one from ten minutes ago.

Vanessa:

Are you going to sleep all day, sleepyhead? ☺

I smile, knowing she's been awake for probably almost three

hours already. It's cute how much of a morning person she is, how excited she is to start every day.

I send her back a waving hand emoji, and she's off, telling me what she's been up to so far today, what else she's thinking about doing the rest of the day.

Claire:

Lol.

Vanessa:

Sorry. I've been up for a while.

Claire:

I know. ☺ Talk after I have breakfast?

Vanessa:

Lol. I'm about to have lunch.

I send her a heart emoji and then head out into the living room. My parents are both sitting on the couch, both on their laptops. They have the news on mute. It's showing people walking around a European city, with big gaps of space between them. Everyone is wearing masks. The words *social distancing* scroll across the bottom of the screen.

My parents look up at me. "Good morning, honey!" my mom says, smiling.

My dad chuckles. "Nice work, sleeping so late. It's like you're a teenager or something."

I yawn and stretch. "Did you guys already eat breakfast?"

"Yeah, a few hours ago," my mom says. "But help yourself. Last night I put together some little individual containers in the freezer. Each has enough for one smoothie."

I raise an eyebrow at her, and she looks at me innocently. "What?" she asks. "This is still keeping it simple. There is no cooking or boiling or sautéing or blanching or broiling or anything involved. I didn't even look at Pinterest!"

I open the freezer, see the individual containers, and take one out.

My mom watches me. "I already cleaned out the blender, so just dump everything in, put the top on, and turn the blender on."

"Mom, I know how blenders work."

"Sorry, sorry!" she says, but she's smiling.

I open the container. I see some leafy greens, frozen chunks of something orange, some ice. I sniff it. It doesn't smell terrible. I dump everything into the blender, put the top on, and turn it on. I pour everything into a cup, then take a small sip. It's actually not bad! I can tell my mom is trying really hard not to watch me.

"Mom, it's good. Thank you."

I walk over to give her a hug, and she hugs me back, but when I pull away, she has tears in her eyes.

"Oh jeez, Mom!" I say, joking. "It's just a smoothie." But as I look at her, I realize that it's not about the smoothie.

She clears her throat and says, "It looks like I'm going to be temporarily furloughed. But really temporarily, just until this is all over. And it's not immediate. It'll probably happen in the next few weeks. So it's nothing to worry about! Nothing for *you* to worry about. I can pick up freelance, and we have savings. Okay?"

"Okay," I say uncertainly, my brain trying to keep up.

"I don't want you to worry, Claire. That's what us grown-ups get to do."

I nod.

"Okay?" she says again, squeezing my arm.

"Um, yeah," I say. There are a million questions rolling around in my head, but I don't know where to begin. And I don't want to make my mom more upset.

My dad has remained mercifully quiet for this conversation. I look at him, still tapping around on his laptop. "You heard your mother," he says. "Nothing to worry about." He smiles at me, a piece of something green stuck in his teeth, and I wonder how it's possible that I'm related to him.

My mom wipes away her tears and my dad unmutes the TV. I try to listen to what the anchor is saying about a possible vaccine for the virus, but my head is spinning.

My mom is losing her job. Probably. Maybe. But I'm not supposed to worry. Somehow.

Once the news goes to a commercial break, my mom stands up and declares, "I'm going to do some laundry."

My dad salutes my mom, still looking at his laptop. My mom gives me a quick look. "It's fine, Claire. Really. Please don't worry."

"Okay," I say again. Then I go back to my room in a daze, my head whirling.

I sit down at my desk, open my laptop, and then suddenly everything from my Babble post comes flashing back to me. The girl on the fire escape, her seeing me watching her, the way she looked mad, then how she smiled and waved at me. How I can't seem to interact with her in any kind of normal way.

And the other thought that flashes into my mind, making a circle around the inside of my head: *why* did I write the post? Why do I feel the need to give a bunch of people on Babble my awkward noninteractions with the girl across the street? What does she have to do with my life, with my girlfriend, with figuring out college stuff? With my mom possibly, probably, losing her job?

I mean, it doesn't matter. So what if I can't have a normal conversation with the girl across the street. What's the big deal, right? It's not like I have to interact with her anytime soon in the real world.

I think about the comment on my other post about the fire escape girl; someone thinks I have a way with words. That I should keep writing. That I should try again with the girl across the street.

But it occurs to me: Try *what* again, exactly? What is it that I'm hoping to accomplish with this girl across the street?

I look at the picture of Vanessa and me on my desk. I'm just trying to figure out who this girl is. Why I've never seen her before. That's all.

That's all.

I wonder if anyone has commented on my post from last night. Not that it matters, of course. Not that I care, of course. I'll just check really quick, before I start my homework and college research.

I slurp my smoothie as I power up my laptop. I read my latest text from Vanessa about her lunch, and then I open up Babble. I click over to my latest post.

I see the words: *Comments: 5.*

Is there more than one bot following me now? Or maybe even some spammers have joined in? It can't be any actual people commenting, right?

I click on the comments section, ready for another *This review is the best.* Or maybe even *Hi, view my profile* or *I make $6,000 a minute working from home,* but . . . that's not what the posts say. At all. The five comments are all from apparently different people. Like, actual people. Not bots or spammers.

The first comment says, *Getting closer! Sounds like the first chapter in a new story. And I love your writing!*

I read through the rest of the comments:

I wish I had someone cute across the street to crush on in lockdown.

Finally, something interesting to read about.

Ooh, this could be fun to follow?

Don't give up! Can't wait to see what happens next!

Wait, someone else complimented my writing? These comments must be jokes, right? Like, no one reads my Babble posts, much less comments on them. It's probably someone bored at home, pretending to like the posts, pretending to be interested. People have a lot of time on their hands these days, and when people have a lot of time on their hands, they love turning to the Internet. The anonymous Internet. Where anyone can be anyone. Where anything can happen.

And who said anything about the girl on the fire escape being cute? Having a crush on her? It certainly wasn't me. It definitely wasn't me. I was just following a Babble writing prompt, writing about what I saw outside. And then an update, because . . . Well, I don't know why. Because I want to prove to a bunch of strangers how awkward I am, that even in a pandemic, when I have nothing to lose, I can't say hi to someone new, be normal with someone I've never met? That I can't even talk to the girl across the street like a normal person?

I look at my closed curtain. I take a deep breath, and before I can stop myself, I quickly open it, then open the window to let in some fresh air.

10

Posted by Clarissareads:

I knew it was a possibility I'd see her sitting there, but her appearance still jolts me. Or maybe I didn't know it was a possibility. Since I still wasn't sure if she was real. But now I know she is. I think.

Sometimes it can be hard to keep track of what's real anymore. And time. *Time*. It drags. Or maybe it doesn't. It's hard to keep track of one day from the next. What makes one day different from another, when they're all pretty much the same. More of watching the news, hospitals at capacity, our state being shut down to outside visitors. More of worrying about what's going to happen with my mom's job. With everything.

But, now, at least, in this moment that will probably soon blend with all the other moments, the sun is out again today, and her hair is doing that lit-up thing again while she is bent over her book.

I grab the book I just started reading this morning, then crawl out onto my fire escape. It's now or never. I clear my throat, but she must not hear me.

I realize I need to do something, anything, so I finally say, as loud as I can, "HI!"

The girl jumps, then looks up and around, trying to trace where the voice came from. She finally looks across the street at me on my fire escape. She waves, smiles, says, "Hi," and then goes back to her reading.

I talked to her, didn't just stare at her. And she waved and smiled back.

She keeps reading, and I keep reading, and even though I'm really into my book so far, it's really hard to concentrate. I keep looking across the street. I watch her turn a page in her book. I watch her run her hands through her hair.

I catch myself looking up a few more times, but then I finally get back to my book, and soon I'm totally lost in it again.

And then, out of nowhere, someone shouts, "See you later!"

I jump.

It takes me a second to figure out where the voice is coming from, until I look across the street, see the girl. She's waving at me.

"Oh, bye!" I awkwardly yell, my voice an octave higher than usual, just as she climbs back inside and closes the curtain behind her again.

Okay, I was wrong. This moment will definitely not blend in with any others.

Likes: 73

Comments: 11

11

I crawl back inside from the fire escape, look at my laptop. Maybe I should do my homework and college research. And maybe I should do it somewhere else, not by my window, just in case the girl goes out on her fire escape again. So I'm not too distracted looking to see if she's there, trying to think what to say to her without being a weirdo. Trying to figure out who she is. And writing about it all.

Who is this girl and why do I keep letting her distract me? Why do I keep writing the Babble posts? It's just because I don't recognize this girl, I tell myself. I'm just trying to figure where she came from. I'm just being a nosy neighbor. That's it. The people who commented with the thing about the lockdown crush and this girl being cute are just projecting, and fantasizing about what they wish their lockdown was like. Not that I think this fire escape girl is cute, obviously. I have a girlfriend.

Still, I need to focus. I need to do my homework and then start my college research for the day. I pick up my laptop and carry it with me out to the living room.

My parents are in a cleaning frenzy. My mom smiles at me as I sit down on the couch, not showing any evidence of her tears earlier. I stick on my noise-canceling headphones and get started on my essay. Who needs desks with windows anyway? It's good to have a change of scenery.

I go in my room a few times to get different books. Each time I go in there I casually glance out the window, like I'm just checking the weather or something. Sometimes I see her; sometimes I don't. I don't stick around long enough for her to see me, for me to feel like I want to say hi.

I don't manage to get around to looking up any colleges. I tell myself I'm going to, I really am, but I just need a break first. I'm scrolling around online, taking some quiz that is supposed to tell me a secret about my personality but is really just annoying me, and my parents flop down on the couch next to me. My dad flicks on the news. I still have my noise-canceling headphones on, but I can't look away from the flashing TV. There is a chart on the screen, showing the number of cases of the virus around the country. It looks like a lot.

My mom sees me watching, says something to me, but I can't hear her because of my headphones. I slip them out of my ears, say, "What?"

"Oh, sorry, Claire. I was just going to ask if the TV will bother you?"

"No, it's fine, Mom. I'm, um, taking a break from my work, anyway."

"Okay," she says, patting my leg and turning back to the TV.

We all watch the news in silence for a few minutes, learning about how cases are leveling off across the city and the Northeast but remain high around the rest of the country.

The next news anchor is standing in front of a hospital in a small California town in full protective clothing, telling us how the hospital is at capacity. My mom turns to me, tears in her eyes. "Want to make brownies, Claire?" she asks. "I think I've seen enough news for now."

"That sounds like a great idea, Mom," I say quickly.

"Joe, can you turn this off?" my mom says, but my dad is completely absorbed and doesn't hear her.

"Dad?" I say loudly, but he's still oblivious.

The next anchor is outside another hospital, this time one in Florida, and I quickly stand up, grab the remote out of my dad's hands, and turn off the TV.

"Hey!" he protests. "I was watching that!"

My mom and I are both staring at him. "We're making brownies!" she says brightly. Too brightly.

"Oh! I'll . . . help?" he says.

"You'll help by folding the laundry? Perfect," my mom says.

"Um, right," my dad says slowly, eyeing my mom. Then he picks up the laundry basket and heads down the hall to their room.

"So, what kind of brownies do you think we should make?" my mom says, tapping around on her phone. "Wow, brownie recipes sure have gotten more complicated these days. Brownies made with mayonnaise? Oh, what about these? Marbled brownies? Oh, wait, that's two different batters."

As she talks, I dig around in the pantry, and then I pull out a box of brownie mix. "Mom?" I say, holding up the box.

She peers at me over her phone. "You want brownies from a mix? Are you sure?"

"Mom! Remember what I said about keeping things simpler?"

"Right, right," she says. "As long as you're sure, Claire."

"Yes!" I say, smiling. "That grilled cheese you made yesterday was so good."

"Really?" she asks uncertainly.

"Really," I say.

"Thanks," she says softly. "Things are just so hard, you know? For everyone. I mean, they're getting a little better in the city for now, but what about the rest of the country? And it's only getting better because we've been in lockdown. What about when life is normal again, when we start going out again? When Dad and I go back to work again? Not that I'm going back to work anytime soon!"

"Yeah, Mom, about that—" I start.

"Honey, what did I tell you? Don't worry!" she says cheerfully. Too cheerfully.

"Mom, I'm not a little kid. We can talk about stuff. Like, money stuff. Before you said there's a lot of money in savings. Do you mean . . . like, college savings?"

She squeezes my arm harder. "I told you. Don't worry!"

"Ouch, Mom," I say, rubbing my arm.

She laughs and then says loudly, "Let's get started on these brownies!"

And we do, and we follow the directions on the box exactly, and they're delicious. I try really hard not to think about money or college or anything except for savoring the way the chewy chocolate tastes.

Then it's time for my nightly video chat with Vanessa. I head back to my room and see the girl on her fire escape. She's reading again and doesn't see me. I close my window and curtain to cut down on the glare from outside. I try not to feel disappointed that she doesn't see me.

I don't think about it for long, though, because Vanessa calls. Something about her looks different, but I can't quite figure out what it is.

"Hey!" I say waving, taking a big bite of a brownie.

"Hey, babe," she says. "What are you eating?"

"My mom and I made brownies," I say, holding the one up in my hand to show her.

"Oh, did you make those black bean brownies I texted you about?"

"You texted me about black bean brownies?"

"Yes, silly," she says, laughing. "We talked about it too."

I comb my memory and come up with nothing, but Vanessa and I also text a lot and talk a lot. Well, sometimes Vanessa talks a lot.

"So what kind of brownies are they, then?" Vanessa says, looking down at my hand.

"Um, brownies?"

"Right, but what kind? Like vegan, gluten-free? Nuts, no nuts? Frosting, no frosting?"

"Frosting on brownies is a thing?" I say. "Wouldn't that just be cake?"

"What? No! That's an entirely different dessert!" She looks as shocked as if I'd admitted I didn't know who Katniss Everdeen is.

"Maybe we should watch the British baking show again," I say, kidding. "To refresh my memory on desserts."

"Ha ha. Soooo?" she says.

"Soooo?" I say back.

"What kind of brownies are they?"

"From the box? I found some mix in the cupboard."

She's quiet for a second, still for a second. I think maybe the call has frozen, except then I see her blink. "Well, that's . . . different," she finally says, frowning.

"Different? It's still a brownie! My mom has been trying to keep food stuff simpler. She's been really stressed about what to cook. Especially since I'm not going back to school for the rest of the year, and she and my dad are going to be working from home indefinitely. And her job stuff is kinda weird now too. Um, just kinda stressful, I mean. I didn't want to bug her with a complicated recipe." To prove my point, I take another big bite of a brownie, looking right at Vanessa as I chew.

"I doubt you'd be bugging her! We've had so much fun cooking and baking and experimenting in the kitchen together. I bet your mom would love to try stuff like that with you."

"She's my mom. I think I know what she likes and doesn't like," I say, my voice tight. "We had plenty of fun making these brownies. The best part of all is we didn't mess them up, and they're delicious, and that's really all that matters, right?"

She's quiet again, and her eyes are on something above the screen. It's been so long since I've been in her room, like actually been in there, and I can't remember what is above her desk, what she's looking at. Finally, she turns her eyes back to me and says, "You don't need to get so worked up about brownies!" She laughs, but the smile doesn't reach her eyes. "Okay, now that we've got that settled!"

"Okay," I say, confused. How is it that I manage to mess up even the simplest of things? Trying to interact with the girl across the street, and now this. I thought brownies were one of the least uncomplicated things in the world to bake, but looks like I was wrong.

She's quiet, playing with her braids.

"Um, are you okay?" I finally ask.

"Yeah, I'm sorry," she says, shaking her head. "I guess I'm just tired."

"Okay," I say. "Should I let you go?"

"Yeah, that's probably a good idea. Talk to you tomorrow!" she says. She smiles again, but it's the kind of smile she saves for someone she doesn't know very well. Which aren't many people. But it's still a smile I've seen on her face. It's just one that's never been directed at me before.

"Good night," I say, confused. She blows me a kiss, and then she's gone.

I avoid my window and curtain, then lay in bed. I open my phone, think about checking Babble but decide not to. The comments have been nice so far, encouraging and all, but my latest post just proves once again that I can't talk to a stranger in a normal way, and I'm not in the mood to read comments pointing it out to me.

I look up recipes for brownies instead. I fall asleep reading about the best kind of beans to use.

When I wake up the next morning, I instantly feel . . . irritable. Like, before my eyes are even open, I realize something is touching my foot, and I can't figure out at first what it is, and then I open my eyes and I realize it's my other foot. I kick my feet apart, but now my sheets feel itchy against my legs. And the elastic against my pajama shorts is all twisted. I climb out of bed, pulling at my shorts, and I trip over a book and stub my toe in the process.

I kick the book, and it goes sliding across my hardwood floor and makes a loud thump when it hits my bedroom door.

"Claire? You okay?" my mom says outside my room.

"Yes!" I say, much more angrily than I mean to. I take a deep breath. "Sorry, I'm fine."

"It's okay. Maybe some breakfast will help?" she says.

She's right. I'm probably hangry. "Be right there," I say.

It's a Monday, usually a school day, but the teachers need more time to plan for remote lessons for the rest of the year, so today is a day off for us. I grab my phone. It's almost ten, so I know Vanessa has been up for a while. But there isn't the usual good-morning text from her, or any texts at all, actually, telling me anything about her morning so far.

That's weird. She said that she was tired last night. But in the course of our relationship I've never known her to sleep past 8:30, and now it's 9:57. A strange sort of feeling starts in my chest.

Good morning.

The three dots instantly appear, then disappear. I figure she's composing a long text to me, but then . . . nothing.

The strange feeling in my chest is starting to spread, and I feel that same grumpy feeling I had when I first woke up, but I tell myself I just need some breakfast. Things always look better after breakfast.

Except that when I head out to the kitchen to look for my box of cereal, I can't find it. My mom is sitting on the couch, drinking coffee, her laptop open, and my dad is next to her, flipping through channels on the TV, his laptop open next to him.

"Need help finding something?" my mom asks.

"Yeah, where is my cereal?" I ask. "I just opened the box like two days ago."

"Hmm, sometimes Dad puts it in the fridge. It might be there if it's not in the cupboard?" my mom tries.

"Wait, why is Dad putting my cereal away? I always put it away when I'm done with it," I say. My grumpy feeling is making a flare-up, especially as I realize where this conversation is heading.

My dad is oblivious, still with the remote in his hand. He finally picks a channel. I don't know why he picks it, though; it's a blaring commercial.

My mom says something, but I can't hear her over the TV.

"Dad! Turn that down!" I shout.

I try to take another deep breath, but it's so loud, and where is my cereal?

My mom grabs the remote from my dad's hand, but she hardly ever turns the TV on or off and always forgets how to use the remote. She fiddles with it for a second, then gets up and pushes the button on the TV to turn it off.

"What was that for?" my dad asks. "I just found an old World Series game. I work better when I have background noise."

"Where is my cereal?!" I yell.

My dad looks surprised to see me and see how mad I am. "Your cereal? I'm sorry, was your name on it?" He grins, proud of himself.

My mom warns, "Joe . . ."

I'm breathing hard, and I feel like smoke is about to come out of my head.

My dad looks a little scared, and then he quickly says, "I'm sorry! It's just so good, those granola chocolate chunks. It's a perfect after-dinner snack." I start to open my mouth, but he says, "We can get more at the store. We'll get two boxes this time. Three!"

I feel like I want to scream, so I'm really surprised when I speak that even I can hardly hear my own voice. "No, we can't!"

My dad says, "Um, Claire, can you speak up a smidge? I didn't quite hear that." He still looks a little scared.

And then it's like all the annoying things that have happened in the twenty minutes I've been awake, including my girlfriend not texting me, all hit me at the same time. And then, I'm like a volcano erupting.

"WE CAN'T GO TO ANY STORES, REMEMBER?! UNLESS WE WANT TO WAIT OUTSIDE FOR WHO KNOWS HOW LONG, WHICH WILL JUST INCREASE OUR CHANCES OF CATCHING THE VIRUS."

"Well, that was louder," my dad says.

"Let's put some in the online grocery cart right now, okay? Let me see how soon a delivery can be made. We're running low on some other things, anyway," my mom says. She pulls her phone out of her pocket, starts tapping around. I watch her, trying to calm my breathing, calm my brain.

But then she says, "Oh dear, soonest order delivery is next week," and I stomp away back to my room before I say or do anything else to my parents, because whatever it is, I know it wouldn't be good.

It feels stuffy in my room. Maybe that's why I'm grumpy too. I open my curtain, then my window.

I look out the window, across the street. The girl isn't on the fire escape. I open my laptop, click around on social media, but just feel annoyed all over again. I open Babble this time, read through book reviews, and then, finally, I click over to my most recent post.

Eleven new comments? Some of them must be spammers or bots this time.

But, they're not.

Okay, I've got popcorn ready for the next part.

Waving, smiling, and speaking! I like it! Keep us posted with your lovely words!

My lovely words?

Soooo cute! I love a good love story.

Love story?

Whoa, slow your roll. I don't think people waving at each other and saying hi counts as love.

Love? That's a bit of a stretch. But, I'll bite! And I'll read more.

Can't wait to see what happens next!

They speak!!

Following!

Baby steps.

Glad to know I'm not the only person who has trouble talking sometimes.

Hey, no rush, right? The world is pretty much shut down. You have all the time in the world to make a new friend.

A strange fluttery feeling starts in my chest. People are actually reading these posts? People are actually liking these posts? Commenting on these posts? Someone thinks I write lovely words? Someone used the word *love*?

I feel a little queasy suddenly.

This is the most people who have ever read or commented on anything I've ever put on Babble. I feel my queasiness start to mix with something else, and I realize that something else is a little spark of excitement.

But then I snap out of it. Love? I love my *girlfriend*. I don't even know who this girl across the street is. I really was just trying to be friendly! Still, now I feel guilt tugging at my stomach. Guilt, excitement, queasiness . . . it's too much to feel too fast. I close my laptop, suddenly wishing the Internet didn't exist.

Obviously, I need to tell Vanessa about this story. About the fire escape girl.

But what is there to tell? That I went out on my fire escape and waved at someone? That I wrote a couple little Babble posts about it?

I pace around my room, pick up my phone. Still no word from Vanessa. My grumpy feeling is even worse than before. So much for Babble being a good distraction, making me feel better. I feel my phone buzz in my hand. A text from Vanessa. Finally!

Vanessa:

Hey, sorry for not texting yet. How's your day?

I want to tell her it's horrible, that everything is annoying, that my dad ate all my cereal, that I'm worried about our family having enough money, that I've been writing these silly Babble posts about this girl across the street and I don't know why . . . but, suddenly, seeing her name on my screen, I feel a little better.

Claire:

It's okay. You okay? Did you sleep in?

Vanessa:

Yeah.

But I don't know which one of my questions she's answering.

While I stare at my screen, trying to figure out what to write back, she is calling me. I don't know why, but I look across the street. The fire escape girl still isn't out there.

I tap the button on my phone to answer, and I see Vanessa's face on video chat, and the rest of my grumpiness from the morning fades.

She looks at me, her hair now loose around her shoulders. I'm waiting for her to say something. Maybe an apology? But what would she apologize for? I'm the one who sucks at cooking, at trying new recipes. I'm the one who sucks at lockdown.

She looks so serious. I know I should ask her what's wrong, ask her why she didn't text me all morning, why she was so quiet last night on our call, but I suddenly feel tired. Not just tired. Weary. Of lockdown. Weary of everything.

And I'm so used to following her lead, her being in charge. Oh god. Maybe she's calling me to break up with me. She's finally realized how much better of a person than me she is, how much better she can do than me.

Finally, she speaks. "My mom's aunt died. From the virus. We just found out this morning."

"What?" I say blankly.

"She got sick. She died."

I don't know anyone who has ever died. Like, no one I'm close with. My grandparents are all still alive and well. My parents both have pretty small families. I feel completely ill-equipped for what to say. Even more than I usually do. "I didn't know your mom had an aunt" is what I finally come up with.

Vanessa gives me a horrible look. "What?"

"I mean, I'm so sorry. For you. And your mom. This must be really hard."

Vanessa sniffs, and I see tears in her eyes. "I haven't seen her since I was a kid. My mom last saw her a few years ago when she went down to Florida."

"So you weren't close with her?"

She looks at me, and I realize I've said the wrong thing. Again.

"I mean, is anyone close with their great-aunt, Claire?"

I have a feeling that whatever I say next is going to be wrong, so I keep my mouth shut.

"This isn't about me. It's about my mom. I hate seeing her so upset, so sad. It's the last living relative she has on her dad's side. Aunt Mable is eighty-four, was eighty-four, so it's not like a huge shock, but still. She got sick a few weeks ago, and it seemed like she was finally getting better. Then she just went downhill, fast, over the last few days."

"I'm really sorry," I say. But something else is bugging me. Besides my inability to ever say the right thing.

"Thanks." She sniffs, wipes her face with a tissue.

"So she was sick for a while?" I say, trying to get my brain to play catch-up.

"Yeah. She went to the doctor because she had this cough that wouldn't go away, but then she got admitted to the hospital right away. I mean, I guess one good thing is she lived by herself. Pretty amazing, to be eighty-four years old and live on your own like that. But at least she wasn't in an assisted-living place or nursing home or anything. Those places are such vectors for this virus. I mean, not a good thing, but you know what I mean, right? One silver lining, I guess is what I mean."

"Right," I say. "So, wait, you knew she was sick for a while?"

Vanessa looks surprised and a little annoyed. "Yeah. Didn't I just say that?"

"You did," I say carefully.

"Babe, where are you going with this?" Vanessa says, rubbing her head.

"I mean, if she was sick for so long, I guess I'm just wondering why you didn't tell me?" I finally spit it out. I think I'll feel better, to finally get what was bugging me off my chest, but when I see the look on Vanessa's face, I immediately feel worse. And immediately wish I could snatch the words and put them back in my mouth.

"Wow," she finally says.

"What?" I say, though I already know I don't want the answer.

"Congrats on making someone else's death about you. That's a real special talent," she says.

"Wait, Vanessa, I'm sorry!" I try, but it's too late. She's hung up.

I try calling her back, but she doesn't answer. I text, but no response. Before this lockdown, we never really fought. I mean, sometimes we got a little snippy with each other, usually her with me if I zoned out during one of our conversations, but usually a shoulder bump or a handhold could make it better somehow. Simple touch. She's never hung up on me before. I wonder how the conversation would have gone if we could have had it in person, if there were no virus, then remember if there were no virus we wouldn't have needed to have the conversation in the first place.

And then, I'm crying. It's like my anger and frustration were a huge glacier that melted and turned into tears, and now I just can't stop crying. And I don't even totally know why I'm crying. For Vanessa's great-aunt? For the guy down the street who used to feed the cats? For everyone dying everywhere? Because I can't go to school? Because of my mom's job and what it might mean for money for our family? Because of my fight with Vanessa? Because I miss her, seeing her in person, touching her?

I realize it doesn't matter, though. I realize nothing matters.

I stick my face into my pillow, scream. I feel better for a second, but then there is a knock on my door.

"Honey? You okay?" It's my mom.

I sniffle. "Yeah, sorry, just frustrating homework."

She waits a second, then says, "Well, if it's more than homework, you can talk to me or your dad, okay?"

"Who said my name?" my dad says, right outside my room too.

I groan. "I'm FINE, guys, okay?"

I hear them whispering, and for not the first time I wish I weren't an only child. They have way too much time to focus on just me.

Finally, my mom says, "Well, come out when you're ready. I'm making nachos for lunch, if that's okay?"

My stomach gurgles at the word *nachos*, reminding me I haven't eaten yet today.

"That sounds great, Mom. I'll be right out," I say.

They whisper some more, and then my mom says brightly, "Okay, honey, see you soon!"

I blow my nose a few times, then head to the bathroom and splash some water on my face. I brush my hair, too, put on some lip gloss, and I look . . . like I've been crying.

I take a deep breath and head out into the kitchen. My parents are sitting at the table, talking in low voices, and when I walk out, my dad jabs my mom with his elbow.

"Ow!" she says. "What was that for?" Then she sees me. "Oh! I wasn't expecting you so soon! I'll finish up those nachos right now!"

"Okay, thanks, Mom."

"And, Claire, come talk to your old man," my dad says. He gets up from the kitchen table and takes the few steps over to the living room, where he sits down on the couch. He pats the spot next to him.

I see my parents exchange a meaningful glance as I sit next to my dad.

"Listen, I don't want to be nosy," my dad says.

"So then—" I start to say, but my dad puts up his hand.

"Let me finish," he says.

"Sorry," I say.

"As I said, I don't want to be nosy, but we really like Vanessa a lot. If you guys are fighting or having troubles, I know you can work it out."

"Um, thanks?" I say, starting to squirm a little.

"Your mom said I should give you girl advice, so here's my advice—just give Vanessa some space."

"Okay?" I say.

"It might feel like you're ignoring her, and she might accuse you of it later, but just give her space, okay? Just hide your phone if you need to!"

"Okay?" I say again.

"And—" he starts to say, but then the smoke alarm goes off again, and we hear my mom slamming around the kitchen.

"I think your mom needs some help," he says over the alarm. "Just remember—space!"

"Thanks, Dad!" I yell, feeling more confused than ever.

They eventually get the smoke alarm off, and we eventually eat some nachos. The ones on the edges got pretty burned, but the ones in the middle aren't too bad.

My parents keep looking at me, then each other, as we eat. My mom clears her throat. "Do you want to watch a movie with me? Your choice! We could even rent one, not just stream one for free."

"Really?" I'm still trying to process my dad's advice about Vanessa, so maybe a movie will be a good distraction.

"Yeah! Anything you want!" my mom says eagerly. Maybe a bit too eagerly.

"Okay, um, let me grab my phone and think for a second," I say.

"Uh-nuh-nuh-nuh," my dad says. "Remember what I said about space!"

"Oh, right," I say uncertainly.

"Oh, good, I'm so glad you guys chatted," my mom says, beaming. Then she hands me the remote. "Anything you want at all, honey."

I pick the first thing that looks not terrible, some action-adventure thing that came out a long time ago. Turns out it's part of a trilogy, so we zone out to the TV for the rest of the day.

And I mostly take my dad's advice. Like, I don't text Vanessa first, but when I stop by my room on the way back from the bathroom after dinner, she has texted:

Vanessa:

That sucked. I'm sorry. Let's talk tomorrow.

Claire:

It did. It's okay. Talk to you tomorrow.

And that feels like following my dad's advice, I think.

12

Posted by Clarissareads:

It's been a rough day. I mean, the last thirty-five days have been rough, but this one was especially hard. And it seems like I'm not the only one who had a rough day. After I finish getting ready for bed, I head back into my room, look across the street. My eyes are so used to following the path to where the girl sits on the fire escape. She's there. She's there! But something seems...not right. Her body is usually so open, but now she's curled up in a ball. And, the worst part, her head is down. Maybe she's just really tired? I look at her hair covering her face, and I'm not sure why, but I wonder what her hair smells like. Probably because I haven't smelled much outside of my apartment in over a month.

Suddenly, she lifts her head, and I forget about her hair, because she's too far away for me to see her tears, but I can tell she's crying.

Must be something in the air today to induce crying.

She rubs at her eyes, sees me, and waves.

I pull open my window, and before I even know what I'm doing, I pull myself out to my fire escape. I say, "Are you okay?"

She nods, but she's still wiping away tears.

"Um, are you sure? Usually when people are okay, they don't cry."

I see her give a little smile, and then she says something, but a huge delivery truck drives by and I can't hear her.

"What?" I ask.

"They're happy tears," she says loudly.

But then she starts openly weeping. Oh god. I have to do something. I look behind me, in my room. I don't know what I'm looking for, what will take away her tears, will take away whatever it is she's crying about. I shout to her, "I'm going to give you my phone number. If you want to talk, not across the street!"

I say it as loud as I can, but she looks confused.

"My phone number!" I yell.

She still looks confused, so I crawl back into my room and get out one of my Sharpies I use for my sketchbook, and I pull out a handful of blank pieces of paper from the pad.

I fill a whole page with the first digit of my phone number: 6.

I quickly fill another page with the next digit of my phone number, and then another and another, until I've written down my whole phone number with Sharpie. Then I tape the pages together and crawl back outside with them, hang them from my fire escape like a banner.

She looks at me, and I shout, "Phone number!" and

suddenly she gives a little smile and nods. She goes back inside, and I think I've ruined another exchange, I've ruined the moment, ruined any chance of helping her with whatever it is she's crying about, ruined any chance of ever talking to her again. But then she reappears with a pen and a piece of paper in her hand. She points at me, at my banner, and she writes something down.

I give her a thumbs-up and say, "If you want to talk! My number."

She gives me a thumbs-up back and heads into her apartment again, and I go back in my room. She leaves the curtain open this time, and I see her sitting on something, either a chair or a bed, and I see her reach for something.

When my phone pings, I realize she was reaching for her phone. Because I have a text from her.

Unknown sender:
Hi.

I've never realized how powerful those two little letters put together could be. *Hi.* Such a small, simple word. Smaller than *hello.* Smaller than *love.*

"Hi." I whisper it to myself, let myself say it louder and louder, until my voice is as loud as it would be for a call with one of my friends.

But this isn't one of my friends.

My phone pings again. Another text. From her.

Unknown sender:
You don't have to do that.

I start to write *Do what?*, but I see the dots; she's already texting more.

Unknown sender:
I mean it was cool of you to give me your number.
But I don't want to be your charity case.

Charity case? What is she talking about?
I look up, across the street, and she's still sitting, looking at her phone.
The dots again.

Unknown sender:
Are you there? I know you are. I see you.

I look up again, and she's looking at me now, waving her phone in her hand.
My thumbs finally wake up, my brain finally wakes up.

Clarissa:
Hi.

Unknown sender:
That's all you have to say? You give me your number and all you say is hi?

I look up, and it's hard to tell, but it looks like the girl is glaring at me. This isn't going at all like I planned.

More dots.

Unknown sender:
Let me ask you a question, window girl. Is this fun for you?

Clarissa:
Texting with you?

Unknown sender:
Oh, she speaks. No. I meant the lockdown. Is this fun for you? Because if you tell me about the bread you are baking and how much you like your pajama pants and your Netflix, we don't need to talk anymore, okay?

Clarissa:
Well, we haven't really talked much so far.

To my amazement, she writes back a smiley face.

Unknown sender:
☺ Fair point. But don't go making me smile until you answer me. Is lockdown fun for you?

I think. Is it nice not having to wake up super early every day, walk to school every day, deal with all the annoying-ness of high school every day? Wonder if today could be the day someone decides to call me a lesbo, or call my friends lesbo wannabes? Like, what does that even mean?

Man, it is nice not dealing with that. So nice. But also, well, a lot of people are dying. A guy a few blocks over. One of my teachers' grandparents. And countless others who I don't know, who live close to me, who live far away. And no one really knows how to make it stop, or when it's going to stop. Or if it's going to stop.

I think back to when I heard that school was going to be closed for two weeks, then the rest of the year. The sheer panic that spread through my veins, that took my breath away. The way my mom spent the first three days of lockdown crying, the way she still cries all the time.

Clarissa:
No.
It's terrible. It's the absolute worst.

Unknown sender:
Are you being sarcastic?

Clarissa:
No.

And then I look up, and she's staring at me from across the street. I stare back. Finally, she breaks eye contact.

Unknown sender:
Good. Now we can talk.

I thought that's what we'd been doing, but I don't write that.

> Clarissa:
> Good. So . . .
> Hi.

Unknown sender:
Hi.

That simple, beautiful word again.

Unknown sender:
I'm Sadie.

> Clarissa:
> Nice to meet you, Sadie. I'm Clarissa.

I like the way it feels to type her name. So much so that I add her name to my contacts.

Sadie:
Nice to meet you too, Clarissa.
Is this what meeting people is
like now?

There are so many ways she could mean that. Or at least, there are so many ways I can interpret it. Does she mean this is a good way to meet? A bad way to meet? She likes meeting me? She doesn't like meeting me? Are we even meeting?

Sadie:
Or whatever it is we are doing. Not meeting.
Texting.

Clarissa:
It's the first time I've met anyone or texted
with anyone this way.

It's just a statement—a fact—but I still have to push down the weird feeling that is creeping up my chest. What if she thinks I'm flirting with her?

Sadie:
What, you don't go around giving your number to all the crying girls on the block? ☺

She's not flirting, I tell myself. But what is happening?

I don't have time to analyze it too much, because those blue dots are going again.

Sadie:
So, elephant in room. Or elephant on fire escape. Why did you give me your number? Did you want to know why I was crying?

Yes, I want to know, and I want to do something to

make it better. I hate seeing people cry. But I don't want to be nosy.

                              Clarissa:
                    Only if you want to tell me.

Sadie:
Well, aren't you considerate. ☺

She's not flirting, I tell myself again. This is just a totally normal conversation between two people in lockdown during a pandemic. I don't write anything back. The blue dots don't appear. And I definitely don't look across the street.

But, finally, the dots are back.

Sadie:
Well, hopefully you won't regret saying that.

I want to tell her I won't regret telling her anything, honesty is the best policy and all, but I don't.

                              Clarissa:
                              I won't.

Sadie:
Good.

And then she tells me why she was crying. She and her mom were just in the process of moving from

Massachusetts to an apartment a few blocks over. Sadie took a bus to her aunt and uncle's apartment, the apartment across from mine. Her mom was finishing up packing and wrapping up things at her teaching job, but then the lockdown began. It's been more than a month since Sadie has seen her mom, and she doesn't know when she can see her mom again. She doesn't mention a second parent, or any siblings, and I certainly don't ask. She ·talks about her friends, though, and says they are all back home in Massachusetts, and they're tired of listening to her complain about missing her mom, especially because one of them has a grandparent sick with the virus. And she says talking to them makes it all worse, anyway, reminds her how far away she is from her old life, from her mom, from life before this virus. She just realized she could actually go on the fire escape a few days ago, and she said it's now her favorite part of her aunt and uncle's apartment.

She writes this all over multiple texts. When I think she's done, when those blue dots aren't on my screen, I wait a few seconds before replying.

Clarissa:
I'd cry too. Like, way more than you did. Like, ugly-cry, snot everywhere cry.

I sneak a glance up across the street, and her head is back. She's laughing.

Sadie:
Thanks. I needed that.

Clarissa:
Anytime.

And I mean it.

Sadie:
Whew, that was a lot. I need some sleep.

Sleep. I've forgotten about sleep. And time. It's already after midnight. We've been texting for almost two hours.

Clarissa:
Me too.

I'm about to put my phone down, but there's another text from her.

Sadie:
Um, don't think you are off the hook so easily. I want to hear about you tomorrow.

Clarissa:
About . . . me?

Sadie:
Yes, you! I know I was doing a lot of venting, but I

don't want you to think I'm one of those people who only talks about themselves.

Clarissa:
Isn't that what you're doing right now?

Sadie:
Haha.
Good night.

She closes the curtain, and I close mine, and I flop onto my bed, wondering what I've just started.

Likes: 310

Comments: 37

13

When my alarm wakes me up the next day, something else has replaced that irritable feeling I couldn't shake yesterday. Something . . . good. I stretch in bed, and when my feet bump into each other, I don't want to crawl out of my skin. When I get out of bed, I don't trip on something on my floor, don't stub my toe on anything.

I pick up my phone, and as I stare at it, trying to figure out how much time I have until my first class, a text pops up from Vanessa. Instantly the good feeling is gone, replaced by something else entirely. As I read her text, her apologizing, her saying how hard everything is, her saying she wants to talk to me, I realize the feeling I have is guilt.

I tell her I want to talk to her too. And I do. I really do. But our first video classes are about to start, so I know it'll have to wait.

Claire:

Video chat at lunch break?

Vanessa:

Yes.

I quickly check my email and social media, saving Babble for last. I click on my latest post and—

Thirty-seven comments?!

Oh my god.

I skim through the comments as I brush my teeth.

Yay!! I knew you guys would connect.

I think I might have goose bumps? Man, I miss having a life.

We know her name at last!

The plot thickens.

Okay, I was a little nervous at first, like Sadie was being all rude, but glad she redeemed herself.

Do you blame her for being rude?? Clarissa had a major staring problem, AND Sadie hasn't seen her mom in forever.

Can't wait to read moooore!

They have each other's phone numbers?! That's a huge step!!

What next, what next, what next?

I think Sadie has a crush on Clarissa.

I think Clarissa has a crush on Sadie.

Edge of my seat here for the next update!

I want a lockdown crush . . .

Oh. My. God. I shake my head, try to focus. I don't have time to read any more comments, think about the post, or anything really—not if I want to eat. I go out to the kitchen and grab a granola bar. As I'm opening the wrapper, my dad walks out from his room, still in his pajamas.

"There's my girl!" he says, and tries to give me a hug. I pull back, though, catching a whiff of his morning breath. "Sorry! I was just so excited about our little chat yesterday. You know we can talk about Vanessa—about anything—anytime, right?"

"Yeah, Dad, I know," I say impatiently. My mind is still spinning, and I need to get dressed before school.

"You just give Vanessa a little more space for a few more days, a week, tops, and I guarantee things will be back to normal, maybe even by next weekend," he continues.

"A few days? Next weekend? That's a really long time, Dad."

"What's a long time?" my mom asks, coming out of their room. She's already dressed.

I look at my dad, and he's beaming. "Remember when we had our little father-daughter heart-to-heart? When you told me to give Claire girl advice?"

My mom pours coffee into a mug. "Yeah," she says slowly, uncertainly.

"I told her all about space, how important it is to give in relationships. How that's probably what Vanessa needs," my dad says, clearly very proud of himself.

"Right . . ." My mom seems skeptical. She looks at my dad's bedhead, his Bart Simpson pajama pants. "Sometimes we could all use a little bit of space," she says quietly into her mug.

"Exactly!" he replies, oblivious. "A few more days of not talking to

Vanessa, a week, tops, is what I told Claire, and things will be back to normal with them."

My mom starts coughing and ends up spitting out her coffee. "I'm sorry," she says, cleaning herself up with a napkin. "You told Claire not to talk to Vanessa for a few *days*?"

"Yeah!" my dad says, starting to look a little uncertain. "Or up to a week. It worked with you."

"Oh, really," she says, crossing her arms. "When was that?"

"When you studied abroad in college? We didn't talk for a few weeks."

My mom rubs her eyes. "That's because we couldn't, Joe. We weren't fighting. We just didn't have cell phones then, remember? And we ran out of money for phone cards."

I check the clock on the microwave. Only a few more minutes until my class starts. "This has been a great chat, guys, but I'm going to get dressed."

"Nice one, Joe," my mom says.

"What? That was pretty solid advice!" I hear my dad say as I close my bedroom door.

I get myself dressed and ready for school. Just three more classes until I can talk to Vanessa. Maybe I can read through some more comments, try to process what everyone said about my recent post then too. I can do this.

I open my laptop, open my curtain, open my window . . . and the fire escape across the street is empty.

But I don't have time to think about it, about anything, because my American history teacher is off and running with her lesson.

Somehow my morning classes fly by. And somehow I manage to focus on them, not just look out my window at the fire escape across the street the whole time. Not, of course, that I care if Sadie is out there or not. I'm just curious, trying to figure out her schedule, that's all. Trying to figure out what that conversation, what my Babble post, was all about.

And then, finally, my forty-minute lunch break.

Vanessa:

Are you ready?

Claire:

Yes.

Almost immediately, I get a video-call notification, and when I accept it, I notice how tired she looks.

"Are you okay?" I ask. It's disorienting to see her look anything but alert and happy.

"I'm so sorry," she says, and then she starts to cry.

"No, I'm sorry. About your great-aunt. About making you upset. About never saying the right things." I fight back my own tears. I feel like I should apologize for Sadie, too, since Vanessa doesn't even know Sadie exists, but also for the Babble posts, since I don't think she knows I'm on there, that I'm active on there, that I'm writing posts. But it doesn't seem like the right time. And Sadie is a friend. Just a friend. I try to focus on what my girlfriend is saying.

"You just did," she says, wiping her cheeks.

"Really?" I feel slightly relieved, but more than slightly guilty.

"Really."

"At first I just thought maybe you were mad about the brownies," I say without thinking.

She looks surprised. "What brownies?"

"The ones my mom and me made."

"Why would I be mad about the kind of brownies you and your mom made?" she asks, confused, wiping her cheek.

Now that I've said it, I realize how ridiculous it sounds. "I don't know. You just seemed mad at first."

I catch myself looking out my window, toward the fire escape across the street, but I can't see anything. Or anyone. I try to shift around for a better view, but then Vanessa starts talking again and I look back at the screen, trying to concentrate on my conversation.

"Well, I wasn't, obviously," she says.

"Right, obviously."

And we just look at each other. I stay focused on my screen, don't look out my window at all.

"I really am so sorry about your mom's aunt. Your great-aunt," I finally say.

"Thank you. I'm sorry too. I'm sad she died, of course, and sad for my mom. It's just . . . this is all so . . ."

"Hard," I offer. "So hard. This new life we're living. I know; we're healthy, we're young. And I'm still really sorry about your great-aunt. I'm not trying to take away from that at all. But it can still suck for us, right? Like, I think we're still allowed to be upset about this. Right?"

Vanessa looks like she's considering what I've just said, but she doesn't say anything yet.

"Look," I go on, "I miss you. So much. And not knowing when we can see each other again? It's just crummy. More than crummy. And like I'm just thinking about other families, separated, who can't see each other. And it just makes me sad." I know this would be the perfect time to tell Vanessa about Sadie, who can't see her mom, but I don't. It feels physically impossible for some reason to let myself talk about her.

Vanessa looks surprised. "That might be the most I've ever heard you say about anything!" I think she means it as a compliment, but I don't like how it makes me feel. I'm trying to think what to say, how to tell her that, but she keeps talking. "Anyway, yeah, I think we're allowed to feel sad. I feel like we're still allowed to feel our own pain, right?"

"Exactly," I say. "It's really, really hard not seeing you in person. Not knowing when I can see you again."

"I know, babe. I miss you too."

"It's not just missing you. Which, believe me, I do. These video chats are just so . . . hard. And if there is no end in sight? It makes everything even harder."

"What do you mean, *hard*? Is your service not good? I've gotten pretty lucky so far with my reception. I'm glad my dad upgraded the Internet speed when he did!"

"No, the service is fine," I say. "Sometimes the video chats can just be a little . . ." I try to think of the right word.

Vanessa looks confused. "A little what?"

"Unsatisfying?" I try. As soon as the word escapes my mouth, I realize it was the wrong one.

Vanessa frowns. "What do you mean? Am I not interesting enough for you?"

"No, no, that's not it at all!" I say quickly.

"Okay, then what do you mean, exactly?" she asks, still frowning.

"I . . . don't know." I regret bringing it up.

She crosses her arms. "No, clearly you do."

"It's just . . . sometimes, when the chats are over, I end up feeling worse than before?" Vanessa opens her mouth to speak, but I say, "No, that came out wrong too. I just mean . . . part of what I love about having you as my girlfriend is touching you, kissing you, seeing you. Like, in person. And I can't do any of that, and who knows when I can, and sometimes I feel like the chats remind me of that—what I can't have anymore."

Vanessa exhales hard again. "Well, I don't know what to tell you, Claire. I feel like we're incredibly lucky. To have access to the technology available to stay in touch from afar. I know it's not the same as seeing each other in person, and I really miss that so much—I do. But I also feel like we should be grateful for what we have. It seems like it's way better than the alternative, which would be not seeing each other at all."

"Yeah, you're right," I say. I want to say, *You're right, as usual.* But I don't.

We look at each other over our screens again. Vanessa breaks eye contact first, and I hear her typing something. She's quiet for a second, reading something.

"What are you reading?"

"Just an article about social distancing for people in relationships."

I look at her, waiting for her to say more. "Um, why?" I finally ask. Then it dawns on me. "Wait. You mean we could see each other?" I ask, confused. "Like in person?"

"Mmm-hmm," she says, distracted again, reading something else on her screen. "I mean, we can't go to the movies or anything, but we could go to the park. We'd have to wear masks and stay six feet apart, no touching. Like, going to the grocery store. Or like when you go for walks with your mom, like how you don't get close to anyone."

"Oh," I say. "But do you think it's safe? I mean, I know social distancing is okay for running errands and stuff, but like seeing each other would be different . . . right?"

She gives me a look, and I'm once again impressed and amazed at how much more knowledgeable Vanessa is than me in all things pandemic.

So I look up "socially distant dates," and soon I'm looking at illustrations of different people, all wearing masks, engaging in different kinds of activities. There are masked people walking in a park, masked people sitting on a picnic blanket, masked people on bikes, even masked people on roller skates. They almost look like normal pictures of people on dates, except that all the people are wearing masks, and there are huge gaps of space between them.

I click back over from the articles to Vanessa. She's staring right at the camera. "How long have you been watching me?" I say, feeling myself blush. I don't know why I suddenly feel shy.

She smiles. "Long enough."

I smile back. It's so nice to see her smile at me.

"Soooo . . . what did you read?" she asks.

"I feel like maybe I have some ideas for socially distant dates."

"Oh, really," she says. "What did you find out? How does one go on a socially distant date?"

"Do you own a pair of roller skates, by any chance?"

Her smile starts to fade a bit. "No. Do you?"

"No," I say. "I have a bike, but it's in the basement of the building. And my parents don't let me use it in the city."

Vanessa says, "Babe, no offense, but maybe you're overthinking things? Maybe we could just go on a walk or go to the park or something?"

"Yeah, that's true." I clear my throat. "Vanessa, will you go on a socially distant date with me?"

Vanessa laughs. "I'd love to."

I hear shuffling by my bedroom door, and then I remember—my parents!

"Wait, are you sure your parents are going to be cool with this?" I ask.

Vanessa looks surprised. "Why wouldn't they be? We won't be close to each other. We'll have masks on. We've all been in lockdown."

"Yeah, you're right," I say, but I already have a hunch that convincing my parents to let me see Vanessa is going to be challenging. Convincing my mom especially.

A date with my girlfriend where we can't touch each other or kiss or hold hands or even stand close to each other, where we have to wear masks over our faces. And one I'll have to convince my parents to let me go on. It's not much, but it's all I have. So, I'll take it.

I smile at Vanessa and say, "Can't wait."

"Me neither," Vanessa says. "Today has already been a better day. No matter what, it's a new day, right?"

And it does feel better. It really does. "You're so right."

We smile at each other, Vanessa's blue eyes sparkling, until she says, "Time for class."

I shake my head. "Right, class." We talked for so long I didn't have time to check my Babble post, read any more comments, but suddenly none of that seems important.

My afternoon classes go quickly, too, but I don't see Sadie on her fire escape at all. I don't know if I'm disappointed or relieved. I don't have too much homework, so I manage to finish it up before dinner between texting here and there. Sadie doesn't make any other appearances on her fire escape.

And Vanessa is right—it did end up being a better day, a new day, and it all went so much more smoothly than yesterday. No one ate any of my food, and I feel better after talking to Vanessa on our video chat and texting with her throughout the day, and it feels like things are pretty much back to normal.

Whatever normal is now.

The one thing gnawing at me, though, is that somehow Sadie and my Babble posts don't come up in any of my conversations or texts with Vanessa. Probably because I don't mention her.

But what am I going to say? The girl on the fire escape across the street was crying and I felt bad, so I went out on my fire escape and gave her my number? And I wrote about it on Babble? I mean, that's probably exactly what I should say, but things with Vanessa still feel somewhat fragile, and I don't want to rock the boat. *She's going through enough right now*, I tell myself. Though if I think my conversations with Sadie—my posts about Sadie—are going to cause any kind of waves, or upset her even more, maybe I shouldn't be talking to Sadie and writing about Sadie in the first place.

Then why do I keep looking out my window?

14

I'm trying to draw again tonight. For the first time in a while. It's hard to keep track of time these days. I draw a picture of two girls, both wearing masks. In my head the girls are happy, but I have a really hard time showing the happiness on their faces since I can't draw their mouths. Which makes me consider that maybe they're not happy at all, that maybe they're not smiling behind their masks.

While I erase again and again and again, my phone pings next to me.

Sadie:
Remember me?

Seeing the text sends a little jolt through me. I tell myself it's just because I'm surprised to get a text, that's all.

I start to type something, but she's already written.

Sadie:
Sorry I was MIA all day. Ended up talking to friends back home for a while.

> Clarissa:
> It's okay.

I wonder what her friends are like, what she's like with her friends. And then I wonder why I'm wondering more about her.

> Sadie:
> Is it cool if I call you? My eyes hurt. Too many video chats with them.

Her voice. In my ear.
The thought makes my insides feel a little squishy.
Her voice. In my ear.

> Clarissa:
> Okay.

Then I stand up, looking in the mirror above my dresser, and I have this big, goofy grin on my face. I catch myself and immediately stop. What is *wrong* with me? I've talked to people on the phone before. I talk to my friends on the phone all the time.

When the phone rings, I pick it up and say, "Hello?" like I don't know who it is.

"Hey there," she says, and her voice is there, right in my ear.

"Hi." There's that word again.

"How was your day, honey?"

I hear myself gasp, just as she laughs.

"Sorry, I'm in a weird mood," she says.

"Ha, right," I say, trying to recover from hearing her call me honey, even if it was a joke.

"I guess part of why I'm feeling so weird is my friends back home were saying they might do some kind of hangout? Like, in masks and staying apart and all that."

"Oh yeah," I say. "That's cool your friends might hang out." It seems like a really flat, boring thing to say.

But Sadie doesn't seem fazed. "Yeah. I'm happy for them and all, but also incredibly jealous. I want to hang out with them—with anyone—so bad. It was so hard to see them all today on a screen. It's why I've deactivated a bunch of my social media. Too many reminders of how far away everyone is, how far away my old life is. Too much salt in the wounds, ya know? I've kind of given up on the news too."

"Really? Why?" I say, as if I don't know exactly what she means.

She sounds surprised. "Um, because everything is kind of terrible? Because every time I check the news, things are worse than last time I checked. Because when I check social media I'm reminded of my old life, my old friends, my mom. None of whom I can see. And I don't know when I can see them, and I don't know when I'll be able to hug them, or even get close to them. Should I keep going?" she asks, her voice shaking.

"No," I say quietly. "I think you've made yourself clear."

Then, to my surprise, she laughs. Like, genuinely laughs.

"I'm sorry," she says. "I guess I'm a little sensitive about all this stuff."

"It's okay," I reassure her. "I think we all are."

"Truth."

And then we both laugh. Together.

"Hey, I think I need to go, actually," she says.

"Already?"

I hate that I feel disappointed. I hate that she can probably hear my disappointment.

"Yeah, I'm sorry. I told you, I'm in a weird mood. I think I have too much nervous energy or something. Maybe I should sleep. I don't know. Do you have a hard time sleeping too?"

"Yes, like every night. It's weird that some people are sleeping well right now."

She laughs again, the vibration in my phone tickling my ear. "You're funny. Let's do a video call one of these days."

"A video call?"

"Yeah. Ever heard of one?" I'm not sure, but I think I can hear her smiling.

"Right, yeah, let's do it!" I say, trying to sound enthusiastic.

"Cool. I feel like I need to escape to another world,

have another change of scenery, ya know? The walls of this bedroom, even the view from the fire escape, are really starting to get boring. Seeing a new face could be a good distraction from all the faces I can't see. Maybe it'll cheer me up. Who knows."

She wants to see my face. She thinks my face might cheer her up.

"Let's do it," I say, instantly forgetting everything I hate about video-chatting.

"Sweet. How about tomorrow night? Ten o'clock?"

"T-tomorrow night, y-yes," I stammer.

"Cool. Catch you then," she says.

"Okay . . . bye?" I say, uncertain if this means the conversation is over.

I hold my phone against my ear for just a second, but then I get the *beep-beep-beep* sound signaling the call has ended.

I turn over to a blank page in my sketchbook. I start drawing Sadie. No mask. She's sitting on her fire escape, her face up, running her hands through her dark hair. No mask. And it's so nice to draw her mouth, her happiness. I run my finger over her lips. No mask.

I draw myself. I'm pretty tall, one of the taller junior girls. My body is all sticks and lines. I draw my hair. You can't tell how thin and mousey it is in the picture, but it is. Nothing like Sadie's hair, which glows in the sun. I'm pretty sure her eyes are blue. I draw her body. It's hard to tell exactly how tall she is from across the street, but I bet she's shorter than me. Where my body is straight lines, hers is all curves.

In my drawing, I'm reaching out my hand, and I make my arm super long, reaching across the street, almost touching Sadie.

I scrawl underneath, *Long-distance friendship*.

No masks.

It's time for bed.

Likes: 845

Comments: 127

15

I wake up the next morning feeling hot. I open my eyes, and a beam of sunlight hits me right in the face. I didn't close my curtain all the way. I check my phone; it's before six. I don't have to wake up for school for almost two hours. I climb out of bed, close my curtain, and fall back into bed.

Out of habit, I check my texts. Nothing. It's too early for even Vanessa to be awake yet. I click over to my email. Nothing too interesting at first, but then I see an email notification about comments on my Babble posts. I open the email, and it's actually a whole chain of emails about new comments. There are a lot of emails.

I'm suddenly wide awake. I open my Babble page, and, oh god, it fills with too many comments for me to even comprehend what they say.

Probably just bots and spammers, I tell myself. *Has to be a whole lot of bots and spammers.* Still, I start reading.

So happy you're pursuing this new friendship! Or romance?

Digging these updates!

Glad you didn't give up on Sadie, even if she was a little rude at first.

Whatever, Clarissa was creepy at first!

Good luck tonight!!

Whoa, things are happening fast!! Texting, then talking on the phone, and next a video chat?!

Love it!

It's okay. I mean, nothing has really happened yet.

There's always gotta be one.

Hater.

What do you expect to happen?

Did you forget we're all in lockdown?

I've never even talked to some of my closest friends on the phone!

Ooh, I bet this is in NYC? I love that place.

OMG, she's drawing pictures of Sadie?!

Wait, I just realized, it's two girls?

Does it matter?

Homophobes not welcome.

I wish I had a cute girl across the street to look at instead of this boring brick wall.

Oh god. What have I started?

I scratch my head. I can't process all of this. People are interested in my story?

And why do people think there is some kind of something . . . happening? *Romance? Cute girl?* I'm just writing about getting to know someone. Being friendly with someone. I have a girlfriend!

It's too much.

I try to go back to sleep, but I'm way too awake. I think about what Sadie and I were talking about, about how we don't understand how anyone can sleep right now. But thinking about Sadie makes me think about Babble, which makes me check it again. The comments just keep rolling in.

I should just put a stop to this all now. Just shut down my Babble account now. This sudden attention is weird. I've never really liked being the center of attention, and it's odd that all these Internet strangers are talking to me—talking about me—like they know me.

It's also pretty weird I haven't told Vanessa anything about my Babble account or my Babble posts. Not that I've done anything wrong. Still, I should go back to writing only book reviews. But no one read those. This is the most traffic my account has ever gotten! And, I don't know, writing about my conversations with Sadie has made me feel a little better, and it's been a good distraction from thinking about the state of the world, from thinking about how much I miss Vanessa, from thinking about money stuff with my mom losing her job.

And if my posts can make anyone feel happy right now when the world has just turned upside down, then maybe it's not such a bad thing! I'm sure it was just a fluke, anyway. People have such short attention spans. I'm sure this will all blow over by the end of the day.

But what if it's not a fluke? I read through more comments.

More details please!!!

I don't like video chats either.

Soooo, today is your first video chat date! How are you feeling about it?

How *am* I feeling about it?

Guilty.

Confused.

And maybe a little excited?

My phone buzzes, and I snap my attention away from the comments.

Vanessa:

`Good morning! ☺`

I shake my head, focus on Vanessa, and all the things she has to say to me at 7:18 in the morning. As I read about her smoothie bowl, I realize suddenly that her texts are part of what makes my mornings in lockdown okay. Her texts, even if they're just about breakfast, are something I can rely on. Depend on. They make me feel safe.

I'm not sure if Sadie is safe.

Luckily, I need to get ready for school, for my day, and I don't have much time to dwell on any of this.

My classes keep me distracted enough from thinking about Babble stuff too much, and from thinking about the upcoming video chat with Sadie. Things seem good with Vanessa again as we text throughout the day. She tells me how she found the perfect recipe for paella, and that's what her family is going to make for dinner.

I don't even check my Babble page until after school. Which feels like progress. Though I'm not sure toward what, exactly.

Just before my homework date with Vanessa, like literally a minute before, I open up my latest Babble post and skim through some of the comments.

Maybe you should tell her you don't like video chats?

Just lie, tell her you like them. She won't know the difference.

Just a friend, yeah okay, wink wink.

Eeek! Can't wait to hear how it goes!

Goooood luck.

I close out of the post, though, and focus on my homework, on Vanessa. On my girlfriend.

After our homework date, I eat dinner with my family, take a shower. Then I wait for Vanessa to call, like she does every night. When it's almost nine and my phone hasn't rung, I start to get worried. Maybe she's still mad about our weird fight? Maybe she somehow knows about Sadie? Maybe she found my Babble account?

I try to calm myself down.

Claire:

What are you up to?

I see the blue dots, meaning she's writing, and I take a deep, shuddering breath, preparing myself for whatever it is she's about to say.

Vanessa:

Sorry, babe! Gotta skip the chat tonight. Lucy and I are making masks.

Relief surges through me. And also confusion.

Claire:

Masks for Halloween?

Vanessa:

Lol! No. You are kidding right?

Claire:

Yes ☺

No. I am not. But I can't let her know that.
And then I remember, medical masks. Right. Duh.

Claire:

Who are you making masks for?

I'm relieved she didn't figure out I had no idea what she was talking about at first.

Vanessa:

Turns out everyone we know! Lol.

Then she sends a picture back. It's a mask, blue with yellow polka dots. It's actually pretty cute. I mean, as cute as masks can be. Way cuter than the paper thing I wear when I go for quick walks with my mom. And it's made really well. Like, I don't know a whole lot about medical masks, but it seems like something I'd find at a store. Not that I've been inside a store lately.

Claire:

Wow, nice work.

Vanessa:

You like?

Claire:

You seriously made that?

Vanessa:

I did! It's for you. We're going to need masks to see each other. Thought I might as well make them cute.

Claire:

You are amazing.

And I mean it. She is. But I'm also thinking that while my girlfriend is making masks, including one for me, I'm thinking about my Babble account, about the video chat with the girl across the street that I'm going to write about. And that a bunch of people apparently want to read about.

None of which my girlfriend even knows exists. And that my girlfriend is making me a mask for a date I haven't talked to my parents about yet.

Vanessa:

> Aw, thanks. I'm going to mail it to you tomorrow morning.

Claire:

> Wish you could mail yourself.

I try to tamp down some of my guilt.

Vanessa:

> Me too. But hopefully I'll see you soon?

Seeing Vanessa is not even a guarantee. I still need to talk to my parents about it. But it's something. And I'm sure once I see Vanessa in person, things will feel more normal with us again. As normal as anything can be while we're both wearing masks and standing six feet apart from each other.

Claire:

> Yes, I hope so.

Even though I'm not sure if I deserve any hope.

Vanessa:

> Talk to you tomorrow! Back to the masks. <3

Claire:

> Good night.

I start to type, *I have to tell you this funny story about the girl across the street,* but I don't know what else to say, and I can't bring myself to hit send. And besides, I don't want to interrupt her while she's making masks. That would be selfish. She's being a humanitarian, and if I take away her focus from making masks during a pandemic, that makes me kind of the worst.

Though video-chatting with Sadie and writing about it for a bunch of strangers on the Internet might also make me kind of the worst.

16

Posted by Clarissareads:

I dig through my closet. I've been wearing so many pairs of yoga pants lately, but I want to change things up, so I settle on a pair of black skinny jeans, a tank top, and a zip-up hoodie. I look in the mirror until I get the zipper pulled up to the exact right place. I pull my hair back in a ponytail, pinning down the loose front pieces. Then I put on some lip gloss, a couple dabs of mascara, and I'm ready to go. Well, not go anywhere, of course. But ready. Or as ready as I can be.

I'm so nervous. Why am I nervous?

Usually when I'm meeting up with friends, I have a little downtime to psych myself up first. Like, taking the subway or bus or whatever. It's sorta extra time to process and prepare for everything. There is time to transition from me-time to other-person-time. But here, in isolation, it's just...me. In my room. How do I switch from the girl in my room to the girl in my room talking to someone I don't even know that well?

When my phone doesn't ring at 10:00 p.m., I tell myself she has probably changed her mind. Maybe she forgot. Maybe she's chatting with someone else.

And then, at 10:02, she calls.

I take a deep breath, pick up the phone, and start my first video chat with Sadie.

Well, I try to, anyway. Because when I tap the button on my phone, all I see is a black screen.

I do hear something, though. Or sort of hear something. It sounds like static and someone saying, "Ughhhh . . . phone."

"Are you there?" I say, but clearly she's not.

Sadie says something else, but it's garbled.

"I think the connection is bad," I say. "Um, I can't see you."

After another garbled response, I press the end call button. It feels wrong somehow, like I'm intentionally hanging up on her in the middle of a conversation, when she was in the middle of telling me something. But I don't have to worry about it for too long because soon my phone lights up again with another call.

My hands are shaking. I take a deep breath, cautiously tap the button to answer the call, and this time, I see Sadie's face on my phone screen.

Sadie's face. She's so close.

"Hi," I say.

"Hi," she says back. She's not smiling at me, but I don't care. This is Sadie on my phone, in my room.

"Sorry about that," she says.

"Oh, don't apologize," I say. "Might have been my phone that wasn't working."

And just like that, she smiles. Her smile is so much better close up than it is from across the street—even better than I had imagined. Her teeth are all really straight, but there's a little chip on one of her top teeth. I never thought a chip on a tooth could be— Wait, no, I need to focus.

But her smile is so infectious. Like, I instantly feel myself smiling back. And then she smiles super big, and it's a smile fest.

Sadie says something about how old her phone is, how it worked when she'd talked to her friends earlier in the day, how she doesn't understand why it's not working now, and I'm trying really hard to concentrate. But taking in her face so close is really distracting. Up close, I can see that she has a little scatter of freckles across her cheeks and nose. Her nose is actually different than I thought, and as she looks at me, I realize her eyes aren't blue.

She's looking at me expectantly, like she's just asked me a question, when I blurt out, "Your eyes aren't blue!" As soon as the words are out of my mouth, I want to put them back in. I don't know why I thought her eyes were a different color, and I especially don't know why I feel the need to share this bit of information.

"Um, what?" she asks, confused.

"Nothing," I say quickly, trying to recover. "For some reason, I thought your eyes were blue."

She leans toward the camera so I can see her eyes up close. "Nope. Green as the day is long. Is that the right expression? My mom would know. She's an English teacher."

That's when her green eyes, which I've just noticed have little gold speckles in them, fill up with tears.

Oh god. Did I hurt her feelings?

"I'm sorry," she says. "I swear I do things besides cry."

"No, no, don't apologize. I'm sorry I said that silly thing about your eyes."

"What? Oh, that's not why I'm crying." She gives a half laugh. "I wish that's all I had to be sad about. Someone wishing I had different-colored eyes."

"I don't wish you had different-colored eyes!" I say quickly.

"Well, even if you did, it wouldn't make me cry." She wipes a tear away and looks me straight in the eye, challenging me.

"I'm sorry," I repeat. I don't know what else to say.

"It's cool," she says. "I'm just sensitive about mom stuff, ya know?"

"Um, yeah."

She's looking at me, and in the silence I'm aware of her taking my face in. I wonder if I look any different up close than she imagined. I wonder if she imagined what I look like up close too.

I feel suddenly self-conscious—of my face, of myself—and I tug loose one of the pieces of hair I had pinned back, twirl it in my fingers. It's a nervous habit my mom had gotten me to break. Mostly.

"You nervous?" Sadie smiles another one of her big smiles, another one where I can't help but smile back.

"What?" I ask, still smiling. "Why do you think that?"

"Um, because it's pretty obvious? You're all fidgety and playing with your hair. Do you not like video chats? They're not for everyone."

"Yeah, I guess they're not my favorite," I say, and I can feel my smile fading.

"Then why did you agree to one, you silly?"

I shrug. "I don't know. Because I'm a weirdo for not liking them during a pandemic? Because you wanted to do one? Because I wanted to do one to cheer you up?"

"Hmm, and none of those reasons have anything to do with you or your needs, do they?" she asks, smirking.

"Yeah, I guess." I fidget a bit in my seat, looking around my room. I look back at the screen, and Sadie is staring at me.

"Am I just making things weirder?" She runs her hand over the part of her head that is shaved, and it looks so soft.

"No! Not at all," I say quickly.

"Okay, good," she says. "I'm all about open and honest communication. Being direct. I don't believe in secrets. Maybe too much, according to some of my friends. But my dad was a therapist, so I've been learn-ing to talk about my feelings pretty much since I learned to talk. If I'm being too weird or too nosy or too TMI, just tell me."

"Your dad?" I say, trying to keep up with the conversation.

"Yeah, he died when I was twelve."

"Oh, I'm so sorry," I say, which feels like a completely inadequate thing to say about the death of a parent.

"It's okay. Really," she says. And something about the look on her face makes me believe her. "He made me promise I'd see a therapist after he died. He was sick with lung cancer. Weirdest thing, he never smoked. It sucked, and I was pretty pissed. So was my mom. We got in some pretty bad fights for a while, me and her. We were just like drowning in grief. But we both kept going to therapy, my dad's final wish, and things are better now."

"Wow," I say, unsure what else to say.

And then, strangest of all, she laughs. "I'm sorry. I know I'm a lot. I wish I could blame lockdown, but I'm kinda always this way?"

"No, don't say you're sorry. It's great. You're great." I say it without thinking, and I immediately regret it when the words are out of my mouth.

"Well, I think you're great too," she says quietly. "I mean, what I know of you so far!" she says louder. "So, tell me more about you. Ya know, basic getting-to-know-you stuff."

"Oh, um. I'm a junior in high school. Well, I guess I'm almost a senior. The school year is all messed up."

"For real."

"Not messed up enough for me to not think about college, though!" I say it more bitterly than I mean to. She studies my face, but I quickly say, "Let's not talk about it. Really."

She looks at me a second more, nods, and then says, "Message received."

"What about you?" I blurt out before I lose my nerve. "Are you in high school, or whatever?" I don't know why I feel so embarrassed asking her such a simple question.

"Ah, I graduated last year. This was supposed to be my gap year where I worked in coffee shops and figured out which college to go to."

"So, wait, you graduated already, and you don't know where you're going to college yet?"

"Yep," she says, laughing. "And the world is still spinning!"

"No, I didn't mean it in a bad—"

"Relax, Clarissa, I'm kidding. Look, I respect your wishes. I'm not going to make you talk about college stuff if you don't want to, but I will just say this one quick thing: It's okay if you don't have your life mapped out at age seventeen. It doesn't make you abnormal or weird. In fact, I think it's weird when people think they have their lives figured out, like in super great detail, before they've even graduated high school. Like, what if you change your mind?"

"Yes! Exactly! I can't tell you how happy it makes me

to hear you say all that!" I say, a bit breathlessly.

"But you don't want to talk about it, right?" Sadie smirks at me.

I laugh. "Um, yes, right."

"Okay. Well, if you change your mind, let me know." Then, after a moment, she continues, "So, what are your parents like?"

"My mom and dad?" My brain is still absorbing everything she just said about college.

"Yeah. Like, are they strict with you? Super annoying?"

I don't think anyone has ever asked me such specific questions about my parents before. I have to think about it for a second. "They're not so bad."

"Okay, well, that tells me nothing in particular at all."

I laugh. "I'm thinking! My mom is . . . like a mom, I guess." I pause for a second, thinking maybe Sadie is going to interrupt me, but she waits patiently for me to finish. "She's like really caring. Like, she wants us to eat well and be healthy. But she also worries a lot. Especially lately. She's had some job stuff going on." I never realized how hard it is to sum up someone's entire personality in just a few sentences.

"Are you two close?"

I think some more. "Yeah, I guess we are. I mean, I don't tell her every detail of my life, but I know if I really had a problem, I could talk to her. I trust her. I guess I've never really realized that before."

"Hey, that's what I'm here for, to make you have epiphanies about your parents," she says.

I laugh again. I can't believe how easy it is to talk to her.

"What about your dad? What's he like?"

I blow out my lips. "He is . . ." I trail off, trying to think of the best way to describe him. "He's a character."

"A good character or a bad character?"

"A good one! Usually."

"How so?" she asks.

I reflect for a moment. "Well, whenever we used to go to the park—you know, in the Before Times—my dad would always try to, like, call the squirrels."

Sadie looks confused.

"Like, to get them to come over, to get their attention. He makes this clicking sound with his teeth and tongue." I demonstrate, clicking my teeth and my tongue together.

She looks even more confused now. "Why does he do that?"

I feel a giggle bubble up in my chest. "I don't know."

Sadie laughs too. "What is he going to do if the squirrel comes over?"

"I don't know!" I say, laughing harder.

"Like, would he invite the squirrel out to dinner? To a movie? To . . ." She tries to say more, but she's laughing too hard.

"Right? Like, would he and the squirrel start going for

walks around the park? The squirrel can show my dad its favorite trash can?" I can't say any more now either; I'm laughing too hard as well.

Sadie has her head back, laughing. I look at her open mouth, her teeth, especially the one with the little chip, and I suddenly stop laughing.

She looks back at the screen, back at me, wiping tears from her eyes. "Okay, I think that's the hardest I've laughed since lockdown started."

"Same," I say. And I realize I mean it.

I look across the street. It's weird, I almost forgot how close she is to me. I almost forgot that she's the same girl I first saw on her fire escape a few days ago. She's standing by her window now. She looks up, waves at me, and I wave back, then smile at the screen again.

We end up talking for almost two hours. She asks me a lot of questions. It almost feels like an interview. I've only had a couple job interviews, for summer jobs, and those were always super nerve-racking and stressful. But talking to Sadie is the opposite of that. It's just so easy. She asks really interesting questions: If you had a choice, what would be the last thing you'd ever eat before you died? If you could only watch one movie for the rest of your life, what would it be? Who would win in a fight, a bear or a shark?

She listens when I answer her questions, like really listens. She tells me things about herself, too, about how she loves scary movies, especially horror movies, how one day she hopes to get into special effects and makeup, maybe. But she's not making a definite plan for it or any-thing just yet.

When I tell her I don't like scary movies, she tells me I just haven't watched the right ones. She asks if I want to watch one with her sometime together over video chat. By the end of our conversation, I've either changed my mind about how I feel about video calls, or I don't dislike them as much as I thought I did.

And just like that, it's almost midnight when we finally get off the phone.

"Want to chat again tomorrow?" she asks non-chalantly. "I mean, only if you're cool with it. I feel like maybe you're more comfortable with it now. And obvi-ously, only if you're free. I'm assuming you probably do a lot of video calls with your friends too. Or maybe not, since you clearly aren't always super into them." She looks me straight in the eye when she says all this, and her green eyes are so intense I have to look away.

I'm quiet for a second, thinking how much I'd like to talk to her again, how right she is about how comfortable I was talking to her, but then I remind myself to play it cool. "Is it okay if we do the day after tomorrow?"

"That's good with me," she says.

"Cool." Then, before I chicken out, I add, "You're right, you know."

"About what?" she asks, yawning.

"About me being more comfortable on video chats now. Thanks for that."

She smiles. "You are most welcome. See ya later!" And she ends the call.

I ended up pacing back and forth across my room for much of the call. I really miss walking everywhere. Now I'm back at my desk. I look across the street, and Sadie is standing by her window. She waves to me, then closes her curtain. I look at her window and wonder if the last couple hours have just been a dream.

Likes: 1,657

Comments: 348

17

I guess the past few days of not sleeping well have caught up with me, because I somehow manage to sleep through my alarm. I wake up to my mom knocking on the door, asking if I'm up yet, with my phone alarm ringing right next to me. I grab my phone and check the time. Crap! School starts in eight minutes.

I jump out of bed, throw on the first pair of yoga pants I see, and pull a long T-shirt over my head as I run down the hall to the bathroom. I emerge a few minutes later, looking and feeling tired, then grab a banana.

While I wait for my computer to boot up, I read through my texts with Vanessa. It's the usual good-morning exchange, and she asks if I want to talk at lunch. I don't have time to check Babble for any new comments on my latest post before my classes start.

By lunchtime, I finally feel awake. But my stomach is gurgling and I'm starting to feel light-headed, so I wander out to the kitchen for food, and my mom has left a sandwich on the counter for me.

The sandwich is cut diagonally in half, and I see peanut butter seeping out the side. I carry the plate back to my room and take a bite. It's peanut butter and honey, and I realize I haven't had this kind of sand-wich since I was a child.

I'm lost in my revelry when I turn the alerts on my phone back on. I nearly choke on my sandwich.

Hundreds of people have commented on the latest post.

I try to read through some of the comments.

OMG they're in love!!

I literally have goose bumps.

I think I have a crush on Sadie? She's so cool!

I lol'ed at the phone not working thing. Like why does it feel so rude to hang up?!

Look at you, Clarissa, getting all dressed up for your first video call with Sadie.

Glad to know I'm not the only one who has a thing about hoodies being zipped to the exact perfect spot.

Oh this is so what I was waiting and hoping for!

Looks like you just needed the right person to do a video call with.

Phew, so relieved I'm not the only one who doesn't have college figured out!

Soooo when's the wedding?

Duh, you guys should do a socially distant hangout. As friends, of course.;)

OMG, my dad does the same thing with squirrels!

Sadie made me feel so much better about school stuff!

And on and on.

And on.

I've only made it a fraction of the way through the comments when my phone rings with a video call from Vanessa.

I answer, try to say something, but the peanut butter and honey are lodged in my throat like sticky cement. I just wave to her, then take a huge gulp of water.

Vanessa watches all this, her eyebrows raised.

"Sorry!" I finally say. "Wrong tube."

"You okay now?" she asks, looking concerned.

I nod, take another sip of water.

She starts telling me about her morning, her breakfast, her classes. I try to think of a way I can read through more comments on my Babble post without her noticing.

I watch her talk, nodding, saying *hmm*, as I reach behind me for my laptop, which I've left on my bed. I can't quite get it, though, so I try to focus on Vanessa. She's looking at me, and I realize I must have missed a question that she asked me.

"Um, what did you say?" I ask.

"I said, are you okay? Are you still sleepy?"

"Yeah, a little."

"I'm always telling you, you need to get more sleep!"

"I know, I know."

"Anyway, since you were up later than me, and usually are up later than me, you've probably had a chance to see these stories that are trending?"

"What stories?" I ask carefully.

"The stories on the Internet! Like, people writing about their real-life love stories in quarantine. It's like even a hashtag now, #loveinquarantine."

I feel a creeping sense of dread. "Really?"

"Yeah, there's so many. A guy saw a girl on her rooftop and asked her out via drone. Drone! And oh, this other couple's first date was in the park, but they were both in giant bubbles. And then these Babble posts, about these two girls who meet when one of them is on the fire escape, and the other girl sees her from across the street, and then they start texting and talking."

I feel a sense of dread spreading through my body.

"Oh . . . w-wow," I say. "That's all really . . . cute."

"Isn't it? It's so nice to read something actually nice and happy on the Internet."

I start coughing again, even though I'm not eating my sandwich this time. Vanessa is watching me curiously. "You okay?"

I nod, clear my throat. "I must still have some peanut butter stuck in my throat."

"Okay," Vanessa says. "Because you know one of the first signs of the virus is a cough, right?"

I nod, clear my throat again. "Just peanut butter." And a huge side of guilt. Deluxe side of guilt. I should tell Vanessa everything now—that I'm writing the fire escape girl posts, but I don't like Sadie, not like that, I'm just trying to be nice, but the words are as stuck in my throat as the peanut butter was.

"You all right?"

"Yeah, I think maybe I am still tired. I'm feeling a little dizzy. Can I call you back later?" I ask.

"Of course. Feel better. I bet you're still just tired. Let me know how you're doing, though?"

"Uh-huh." Somehow I manage to push the button to end the call.

I put my phone down, look around my room, look across the street at the fire escape, but it's like my eyes can't process it. It's like when I come inside from being outside on a sunny day, and my eyes can't adjust, and everything looks kind of dark.

I miss going outside on sunny days without wearing a mask.

I really want to tell Sadie everything. That I saw her on the fire escape, wondered who she was, and I started writing these Babble posts that were just supposed to be a writing exercise, because everything around me is so weird and scary, and now it's turned into a thing that people apparently want to read—even my girlfriend. Except my girlfriend doesn't know that I'm the person writing the posts.

Things are getting way out of hand, and I don't know how to put a stop to it all. I mean, I do know: I could literally just stop posting, delete my account, and maybe this will all go away overnight. But as much as I hate to admit it, maybe I don't want to put a stop to it all yet. Because I don't want to write about getting in fights with my girlfriend, about seeing my mom cry, about how much I miss seeing my girlfriend in person, about how scared I am over the virus, about how I have no idea where I want to go to college or how I'll pay for it, or what I want to do with my life.

I don't want to think about all that, so I open up Babble and start to scroll through the comments from last night's post. There are still so many coming in.

But I'm done reading comments. I'm done thinking about Sadie. I'm going to focus on my schoolwork. On my girlfriend. On colleges. On researching financial aid. On figuring out a way to talk to my parents about going on a date with my girlfriend. I tell myself all this as my next class starts. I take notes, listen to the teacher, and only look out my window at the fire escape across the street once.

Maybe twice.

After school, I try to busy myself with a post on Babble. A post that has nothing to do with Sadie, but an actual book review. I purposely ignore the comments from my latest posts. It's been a while since I've worked on a review, and I want to write some while the books are somewhat fresh in my brain. It feels good to think about books.

I've just finished and posted my review of Stephanie Kate Strohm's latest, when my phone buzzes. It's been so long since I've written a review that I'd forgotten how much I actually enjoy it, and I've totally lost track of time.

It's Vanessa. Ready for our homework video call.

"Hey, babe!" I say, answering the call with a smile. I feel good. Rejuvenated.

"Well, you look happy," Vanessa says, smiling back. "So much better than before!"

"I am! I was just—" I stop myself. Am I ready to tell Vanessa that I was working on a Babble review? That I'm the one who has been writing the Babble posts about Sadie? I look into my girlfriend's expectant, smiling face and quickly say, "It's just . . . nice to see you."

"It's nice to see you too," Vanessa says softly. "And it'll be even nicer to see you in person!"

"Right . . ." I say slowly.

"Baaaabe, have you talked to your parents yet?"

"No, but I promise I will soon."

Vanessa's smile gets a little smaller, but she says brightly, "Okay!"

I smile back, but it's harder to do now. Smile.

We get to work on our school assignments, and I'm able to concentrate, get through some of my trigonometry homework. I look up once, and Vanessa has her head down. She's rubbing the back of her neck, and I remember what it was like to touch her neck, touch her, her soft skin.

She looks up at me suddenly, still rubbing her neck. "What is it?"

"I . . . I wish I could rub your neck," I say.

Vanessa smiles. "Me too. I have such a bad knot. Too much time sitting in the same position. I'm thinking about getting one of those standing desks."

"Really? I mean, it's the spring. There's not too much school left until the summer break. You want to rearrange your room for that?"

"Well, I'm thinking ahead too. In case there isn't in-person school in the fall."

"Wait, that's a possibility?" I say, trying to keep my voice calm.

"Anything is a possibility at this point," she says calmly.

"But . . . if there isn't school in the fall, then . . . when . . . when can we see each other again?" My eyes burn with my tears, my face feels hot, and I'm having a hard time trying to control my breathing.

"Well, hopefully soon! On our socially distant date, remember?"

"Right, right," I say, but I'm distracted. "But like . . . when can we hug again? Kiss again? Go the movies again? Go to each other's apartments again? See any of our friends again? And if there is no school in the fall, when will it start again? Like, will we ever go to in-person high school again? Will my last day of high school be that weird day last month when Principal Shaffier made that announcement and—"

"Babe." Vanessa is laughing, but I don't know how. "There is no point in worrying about any of this stuff now. My mom always tells me worrying is a wasted emotion."

"I think it's worse than worrying?" I say uncertainly. "I mean, I get worried before a big test. This seems like a bigger thing. Like, it needs a bigger word?"

"Babe, calm down," Vanessa says. "Let's talk about something else. Like, my desk!"

"Your . . . desk," I say, confused.

"Yeah. Distract yourself. Like, there is this standing desk I want to get. Because whatever happens in the fall, I can still use it for homework. But I'm also thinking I'll probably take it with me to college."

"Right . . . college," I say back weakly.

She laughs again, which seems impossible. "It's never too soon to start planning on what you'll need to bring with you. A lot of dorms have desks already, but if I decide to do an unfurnished room off-campus, I'll take it with me."

"Off-campus," I repeat.

"But I don't know, it might be nice to live on campus freshman year. Cheaper, too, I think, based on what I saw on the housing websites for Dartmouth and Amherst College."

"Right," I say again, though I'm having trouble following the conversation.

Vanessa goes on, "You wouldn't believe how much some of these places charge! And like, we live in an expensive place now. But still, I've had some serious sticker shock."

I smile because I don't know what else to say or do.

"Do you think you'll do on-campus or off-campus housing if you get into Dartmouth or Amherst College?" Vanessa asks me.

"Umm . . ." I say slowly.

"Claire, these are things you have to think about."

"I know, but I'm still making my final list of schools to apply to, and—"

"Right, and as I keep telling you, on that list, you should include tuition and room and board. And financial aid. Because even if a school seems like it's not too expensive, if they don't offer any aid, it ends up costing more, ya know?"

I smile, but it feels more like a grimace as I think about tuition, about money.

"You *have* been thinking about college stuff, right, Claire?" Her blue eyes pierce mine, and I feel myself squirming. "Remember, we said just do an hour or two a day of research. That's it."

"Thinking, yes, of course!" I say impatiently.

Vanessa isn't deterred by my impatience. "Babe, this is serious. This is your future. Where you go to college, what you study, is going to affect the rest of your life. Dartmouth and Amherst College are both excellent schools, just so you know."

"I know, I know," I say, trying to quell the impatience in my voice.

"Do you, though? Because I don't really see you taking it seriously. I see you brushing it off, making jokes about it."

"I'm sorry," I say.

"For what?"

"What?"

"What are you sorry for? You said you're sorry."

"I did?"

"Yes!" Vanessa shouts. "I think sometimes you just say it, that you're sorry, and you don't even realize you've said it. It's some kind of automatic thing for you. I almost wonder if it's some kind of deflection?"

"I'm—" I catch myself before I say "sorry."

Vanessa smiles. "Maybe I've been reading too far ahead in my psychology class."

I don't want to accidentally say "I'm sorry" again, so I don't say anything at all. Vanessa just looks at me, waiting for me to say something. But I don't know what to say. About anything.

Finally, she says, "Okay, back to homework?"

I nod.

And we both go quietly back to our work.

After I finish my homework, I have dinner with my family, boxed macaroni and cheese. "It's *organique*!" my dad says.

My mom and I roll our eyes at him and his terrible attempt at a French accent.

Then I go back to my room, talk to Vanessa, say good night to her, and then get myself ready for bed. I should be tired, but I feel super awake. I sit down at my laptop. I think about my conversation with Vanessa, about colleges. I take a deep breath, then type, "which colleges should I apply to?" into a search engine.

I get tons of results, tons of websites. I click around a little, read some of the articles, but soon the words start blurring in front of me on the screen.

I take another deep breath, and this time I type, "which colleges cost the least amount of money." But it just brings up a similarly overwhelming list.

I close the search engine, frustrated. Then I open up Babble. I read over my last book review. And, wow, there are actually thirteen new comments?! I feel a tiny boost of confidence. Maybe I should go back to the kind of writing I originally started my account for. Now I've got a bigger audience, so my reviews can reach more people. Maybe writing about Sadie has just been part of my path, my journey, to becoming an accomplished writer, with actual followers.

But when I start reading the comments, any sense of confidence I had quickly deflates.

Boring!

Go back to the love story.

Snooze.

What's the latest with Sadie?

Ummm, I thought this was supposed to be about a lockdown romance?

Don't care.

And even more, none of them very nice. I sigh, then go back to other posts, Sadie posts. I read those comments.

Love this.

Can't wait to hear what happens next!

Omg, so cute!

Well, I'm hooked!

I sigh again. I wonder if I can pick a college major about being bad at things. Or if there is a college for people like me who excel at not excelling.

18

My phone vibrates on my desk.

Sadie:
You okay? Not trying to be creepy, but when I saw you in the window a little while ago you looked pale. Like I could see your paleness from across the street! You also didn't wave at me. Lol.

Clarissa:
I didn't even see you.

What else have I missed?

Sadie:
Yeah, so back to my orig. question. Are you okay?

Clarissa:
I'm okay. Just tired.

Sadie:
Yeah, me too!
Sorry if I kept you up too late last night.

I start typing, hit delete, and start typing again.

Clarissa:
It was worth it.

Sadie:
☺
It's almost like destiny, isn't it?

The word makes me gasp, and I'm grateful we're just texting, not on the phone or anything.

Clarissa:
What's like destiny?

Sadie:
Oh, just that we're across the street from each other during this crazy time, that's all. Good to know we're not in this alone and all that.

Clarissa:
Right, right.

Sadie:
Have a good afternoon!

Clarissa:
You too.

Suddenly, I feel much better. And I think I will have a good afternoon. It's hard not to when someone uses the word *destiny*.

When a friend uses the word *destiny*.

A friend.

She's a friend.

Likes: 3,512

Comments: 652

19

The next morning, I purposely don't check Babble or my email. It's another teacher-planning day, so another day off from school. I used to look forward to days off from school, when not going to school was different, exciting. What I wouldn't give to feel some of that excitement now.

We haven't done much laundry since lockdown started, just a load here and there, and our hampers are overflowing. We used to use a laundry service, but it seems risky now, so my dad drags our laundry to the basement of our building, and my mom and I fold and put things away. We put some music on, and it's actually not an awful way to spend a morning, go figure. Much better than doing homework or researching colleges.

Finally, when all the laundry is done, I go back to my room and open up the Babble app on my phone. I read through the latest comments:

Well, that's more like it.

UM, Sadie used the word destiny!

Such a short update! But still, better than the book review.

That's it?!

Destiny?!?!!

Aw, Sadie was worried! So cute.

I want a longer post!

Aw, man, don't leave us hanging!

Why was she so pale?

Yeah, everything okay, Clarissa?

Is she sick?

She. As in me. As in people have been speculating about my feelings toward Sadie. Sadie's feelings toward me. These strangers. Strangers discussing my health. These people who don't want me to write book reviews, who want me to write about Sadie. Long, detailed posts about Sadie. Strangers. Why am I letting these strangers—what these strangers want, what these strangers think—affect me so much?

I close the app on my phone, feeling annoyed. I've just gotten back to my room, but I already need a change of scenery, so I head out to the kitchen.

My mom is there, on her laptop, her face scrunched up as she taps away at her keyboard.

She looks up at me, her fingers still typing. "You okay?"

I think about what Sadie asked me, if I'm close with my mom, and how I told her that I trust my mom, and that if I really had a problem, I could talk to her. More than anything, I want to tell my mom about my Babble posts, about Sadie, but I don't even know where to begin.

"Yeah, I'm okay," I say. "Well, whatever okay is these days."

My mom looks at me, clearly worried.

"It was a joke, Mom."

"I'm going to take you at your word. But you know you can always talk to me or your dad about anything."

I think about my conversation with my dad, when he told me not to talk to Vanessa for a few days. "Right," I say, nodding.

"Okay," she says, but I can tell she still doesn't believe me.

"What do you think about social distancing?" I blurt out.

My mom looks confused. "What?"

"I guess I was just wondering what you thought about it?" I say. "Like, aside from just going on walks together around the neighborhood. Like, what about social distancing . . . with other people?"

My mom's computer chimes. Her eyes dart over to it, and she groans. "Ugh, sorry, Claire, I'm interviewing with a potential freelance client. Can we talk about this more later? Are you thinking about school in the fall? Is that why you're asking about social distancing?"

"Um, yeah, that's what I'm thinking about," I say quickly. "School in the fall."

My mom looks unconvinced, but her computer keeps chiming, so she puts on a big smile, then answers her video call.

I head back to my room.

I try to get a start on my homework before my call with Vanessa, but I can't concentrate. I scroll through social media, looking at pictures of Vanessa and me. My profile picture is a picture of us from Valentine's Day. We didn't feel like going out for some overpriced meal at a crowded restaurant, so we ate instant noodles and watched an old movie from the nineties at my apartment. I remember sitting next to her on the couch, running my hands through her hair. How good her hair smelled. I used to find her hair everywhere. In my backpack, stuck between the keys of my laptop, clinging to my clothes. I miss finding her hair everywhere.

Vanessa texts me, asking me if I've talked to my parents about our date, and I have to tell her no. We do homework over video chat; she doesn't mention our potential date once, and then it's dinnertime. And then it's video-chat time with Vanessa after dinner, and we watch a show. She asks me why I didn't talk to my parents, and I try to think of a reason to tell her, but I can't think of anything.

After the show we say good-bye, tell each other we love each other, but I know she's annoyed. And I'm annoyed at myself that she's annoyed.

I know checking Babble isn't going to make me feel any less annoyed, but I check it anyway. It's just more people saying they want to know the latest on Sadie. They think we like each other. They really didn't like my book review. They want to know why I was so pale. They really want a longer post. They think we should hang out. And on and on with the personal, nosy questions, comments, demands.

I tell myself it's all irrelevant. Just people with too much time on their hands with nothing better to do.

We all have too much time on our hands.

When I wake up the next morning, I realize I've left my laptop open on my desk, and little notifications are popping up in the corner. I shuffle over to my desk, tap the keyboard, and the first thing I see is a text.

Vanessa:

> Don't forget to talk to your parents about us hanging out!

And then come the email notifications telling me there are comments on my Babble post. So many emails. So many comments.

Okay, this short little post is cute and all, but I want a longer update!

Yeah, what else are you guys texting?

Destiny?!?!?!

Hey, one thing I just thought of: Does Sadie know about these posts?

Oh snap, good point.

I dunno if I'd think it was creepy or cute if someone were writing Babble posts about me.

She's just writing about their conversations? It's not like she's giving any personal, confidential info away?

I dunno. I'd be creeped out.

Really? I'd be so completely flattered.

Um, Sadie is the one who mentioned destiny, not Clarissa.

Creepy McCreeperson.

Who's creepy, Clarissa, or Sadie, talking about destiny?

I think it's cute.

I still think they should hang out in person.

The comments keep going.
It's too much to think about right now. Too much to process.

I get another text from Vanessa. She tells me she just did some family yoga.

I check the time. It's a little after eight.

> **Claire:**
> What time did you guys all wake up?

Vanessa:
> You know us, a family of early risers.

> **Claire:**
> Lol.

Vanessa:
> It was fun, though. You should try it with your parents.

I think for a second. I know my mom does yoga, used to do yoga, at a studio not too far from our apartment. But I think about my dad trying yoga, and I start laughing.

> **Claire:**
> Lolll, my dad doing yoga.

Vanessa:
> What's so funny?

> **Claire:**
> Just picturing my dad doing yoga, lol.

I really am actually laughing out loud thinking about my big, lumbering, bumbling dad trying to get himself into Warrior 1.

Vanessa:

Okaaay, and?

Claire:

You've met my dad, right?

Vanessa:

Yeah, obviously, and?

Claire:

Don't you think it's funny thinking about him doing yoga?

Vanessa:

Why is that funny?

Claire:

Because he's my dad! My big, clumsy dad, who has less flexibility than one of my pens.

The blue dots start, stop, start. Then, finally:

Vanessa:

It's not very nice to make fun of people's bodies. Every body has their own path, their own journey.

Claire:

I know.

It's way too early for this conversation.

Claire:

Sorry.

But I don't know why I'm sorry, what I'm apologizing for.

Vanessa:

> Make sure you eat some breakfast. You looked so pale
> yesterday. I hope you slept better last night.

Claire:

> Yep, going to go do that now. Talk soon!

I feel annoyed, but I try to blame it on being hungry.

Vanessa:

> Don't forget to talk to your parents. ☺

I put my phone down.

My parents are both in the kitchen, pouring coffee and making breakfast. I pour myself some cereal and actually sit down at the kitchen table today. I need a break from my laptop and thinking about Babble.

My parents sit down too. My dad scrolls through his phone, and my mom kind of stares off into space. It's one of those days where none of us are feeling like morning people.

"Do you think we should try family yoga?" I ask.

My dad doesn't even look up from his phone, and my mom just looks confused. "What do you mean?" she asks.

"Just what it sounds like. Family yoga. We could all do it together. Like, do yoga poses together. Through the TV or computer or whatever."

My mom looks at my dad. "Joe, what do you think about that?" I can tell she's trying to make her voice sound bright and enthusiastic.

My dad looks up. "Think about what?" He's not looking at his phone, but his thumb is still scrolling up and down. The motion reminds me of when a dog is trying to scratch an itch it can't reach.

"Family yoga," my mom says. "Can you please put your phone down when we're talking to you?"

"Sorry! I didn't know anyone was talking to me."

"Probably because you were on your phone!" my mom snaps.

My dad makes a big show of getting up, putting his phone down on the kitchen counter, and then sitting again. He folds his hands in front of him. "Now, what was this about family yoga?" he says, batting his eyelashes at me, then my mom.

"Claire was thinking we could do family yoga!" my mom says, in that fake bright voice again.

"What? Why?"

"It's something we could do together," I say. "As a family."

"Don't we do enough together as a family?" my dad asks.

"Joe . . ." my mom warns.

"Okay, Claire." My dad nods. "If this is something you want, we can do it."

My mom snickers and tries to hide it by turning it into a cough.

My dad and I both look at her. "What?" she says innocently.

"Are you laughing at your dear daughter's idea?" my dad asks, trying to look appalled.

"No, Claire, I would never laugh at you or at any of your ideas. You know that, honey." She pats my hand. "I was just thinking about your dad in yoga pants, trying not to fall over while he does a downward dog . . ." She can't say anymore, because she's laughing too hard.

"Isn't it mean to make fun of someone's body?" I ask.

My mom's eyes are starting to water, she's laughing so hard. "Oh, Joe, I'm not making fun of your body. I love your body—"

"Ugh, gross!" I interrupt loudly.

My dad pops up from the table, walks to the living room. "What? You don't think I can do some yoga?" He bends over, and different parts of his body make cracking sounds. He gets stuck somewhere between a downward dog and a plank, and then somehow he falls over, making a big thud on the floor.

My mom and I crack up, and when my dad finally pulls himself up, he's laughing too.

"Who says I can't do yoga?" He flexes his arms and kisses his biceps. "When do we start?"

My mom and I are laughing too hard to answer. My dad takes the opportunity to try downward dog again and promptly falls over again.

My mom and I both have tears streaming down our faces, and my mom gasps, "Joe, stop! This is important to Claire!"

I shake my head, manage to say, "This definitely isn't family yoga, but it's way better."

I head back to my room a few minutes later, feeling light and ready to start my day. I don't remember the last time I laughed so hard with my parents.

At lunchtime, Vanessa texts me that she's baking bread with her family and asks if we can do a video chat in a little bit.

I tell her sure, and I finish my English essay.

And then I wait for Vanessa.

I click over to my email to pass the time, but it's more comments on Babble—more people, more strangers, talking about me, demanding things of me, talking about Sadie, analyzing all our words. It just feels weird. And more than a little creepy. And also . . . wrong.

I try to start a post. I want to confess everything—that I'm starting to feel guilty for not telling Sadie about the posts, for not telling Vanessa that I'm the one writing the posts; that I've given people the wrong impression, that I have a girlfriend I love; that Sadie is just someone helping me get through a really hard time, and that maybe I'm helping her get through a really hard time too. But it's like I have writer's block or something. I don't even know where to begin.

Maybe it'll just be easier to give these people what they want for now, right? Surely they'll move on from my story soon . . . right?

20

I haven't been sleeping well.

What helps me fall asleep some nights, though— when my lights are off, my eyes wander to the fire escape, to the window across the street. Whenever Sadie is in her room, when she's awake, she looks across the street at me and waves. It's become so normal to see her there, so familiar ... so comforting. Comfortable. It helps me sleep. Because that's what friends do for each other, help each other fall asleep.

But now it's daytime, and I can see Sadie across the street. She's on the fire escape, phone in her lap. She doesn't notice me. But that's okay. Just seeing her somehow makes things better, at night and during the day.

A text from her pops up in the corner of my laptop screen. So wild to see her across the street, to know that her phone was out because she was texting me. That now her words are in my phone.

Sadie:
You still cool to chat tonight?

Clarissa:
Yeah, if you are!

And for once, I'm not lying about wanting to do a video call. She's fun to talk with. She's a fun friend to talk with.

Sadie:
Cool, what time is good for you?

Clarissa:
Is 10 again okay? Too late?

Sadie:
Too late for what? ☺

Clarissa:
Haha.

She's just a friend, just joking around with me.

Just a friend.

Just a friend.

Seeing her and talking to her just makes things better.

That's what friends and friendships do, right?

Sorry if this post isn't long enough, detailed enough, for you, my readers. ;)

More soon!

Likes: 2,353

Comments: 654

21

My phone rings with a video call from Vanessa. I run out to the kitchen, grab the sandwich my mom made for me for lunch, and answer her call back in my room.

"Please tell me you talked to your parents!" is the first thing Vanessa says to me.

"About what?" I ask, smiling sweetly. Oh my god, lockdown is definitely turning me into my father.

Except Vanessa isn't amused. "Claire, do you even *want* to see me?" she asks. I think I see the smallest of pouts in her bottom lip.

"Yes, of course I do," I say. "I'll talk to them."

"Okay," Vanessa says uncertainly. "But seriously, I'm not bringing it up anymore!"

"Okay." I feel slightly relieved. One less way for me to worry about disappointing her. "Oh, so we tried some family yoga!" I say, trying to change the subject quickly.

"Really? When?"

"This morning," I say. "We tried some at breakfast. Well, my dad did anyway. But he just fell over. It was really funny." I laugh a little to myself, thinking about it.

But once again, Vanessa doesn't look amused. "You and your family love turning things into jokes!" she says tightly.

"It was my dad!" I protest, but I'm smiling.

"Anyway." She still doesn't look amused. "What do you have for lunch?"

"Peanut butter and honey sandwich," I say, holding it up. I take a bite. "I don't know why, but it always tastes better when it's cut diagonally."

Vanessa is making a face at me. "Can you try telling me that again when your mouth isn't full? You know I have that thing about the sound of food being chewed."

I want to remind her that this lunchtime call was her idea, but I don't want to talk with my mouth full again, so I just hold up the sandwich, show that it's cut diagonally.

"Oh, cool," Vanessa says, clearly not in the least bit impressed.

I'm still chewing, so I gesture to her, to her lunch, for her to show me what she has.

She looks at me for a second, trying to figure out what I'm doing, then holds up her bowl. "It's toasted quinoa with roasted root vegetables and a sesame dressing that we made."

"Oh."

"Yeah," she says. "We all made it last night."

Then we just eat our lunch and look at each other until we're done eating. I'm too busy concentrating on chewing and not talking at the same time to think about why Vanessa is being so quiet with me.

Vanessa is true to her word. She doesn't ask me again if I've talked to my parents about hanging out with her. I feel a little guilty, but I also just can't find the right opportunity to bring up the topic with my parents. So I don't.

I know I should ask Vanessa if we're okay, but I'm so used to her taking charge in everything, it's really hard for me to bring anything up with her. So I don't.

A little bit after 9:00, Vanessa tells me she's tired and going to bed. Which is earlier than usual, and I feel like I should say something about that, but I don't know what to say. So I don't. We say good night to each other and hang up.

I want to ignore the emails about more comments coming in on my Babble posts. I really do. But curiosity killed the teenager, I guess, because I start reading. And immediately regret it.

Boring.

Um, yeah, she joked about her last post being too short . . . and then wrote another short post!

This tells us NOTHING! We already know she can't sleep, duh.

Internet trolls. Nothing better to do than hate on something that has nothing to do with them.

Not a troll here. I just think it's weird that we don't know who these people are. Like actually know specifics.

Maybe Clarissa wants to be anonymous?

Maybe it's all fake? It's a story, after all . . .

Why be anonymous tho? What is she trying to hide?

What if Clarissa is really some old gross guy in the middle of nowhere?

I think we need to hear if Sadie has anything else to say about destiny.

I bet the next post will be more interesting.

Clarissa, prove you're real!

Guys, chill out. Enjoy the posts.

Seriously. Fun ruiners.

I think we need a picture of Clarissa. To prove you're real.

I think you guys need to get a life.

Picture, or it didn't happen.

I shiver, even though it's not cold in my room at all. These comments have suddenly gotten really creepy. Why do these Internet strangers think I owe them something like a picture of myself? Why do they think they deserve anything from me? I don't have any idea who these people are; they don't need to know who I am. They could be . . . anyone. *I* could be anyone.

Anyone can be anyone online.

22

I have a video call with Sadie in five minutes.

Even though it hasn't been that long since our last call, and she is right across the street, I feel like I missed her or something. It's weird.

I don't change my clothes, don't do anything different with my hair, and I definitely don't bother with any lip gloss or mascara. So when she calls, I'm in the same yoga pants I've been in all day, the same old vintage shirt that used to be my mom's.

I answer the call, and there she is. She's smiling. At me. That little chip in her tooth. And how have I forgotten how green her eyes are? I mean, it's just remarkable, the technology, that her eyes can look so green over a screen.

"How's it going?" she asks.

I force myself to focus. On speaking. Not on looking at her. I clear my throat, and I answer honestly. "I mean, I guess not terrible, considering we're in the middle of a pandemic."

She laughs. "Right? It's so weird to me when I'm talking to my friends back home, and like, if I ask one of them how they are, and they say they're great? Like, how is it possible that anyone or anything can be great right now?"

"Yes, exactly!" I say. "I freaked the heck out when I found out there wouldn't be any school for two weeks, and I freaked out even more about the rest of the year, and everyone thought I was overreacting both times." The last part kind of slips out. I hadn't planned on saying it when I opened my mouth.

Sadie makes a face. "Are you serious? I don't think it's possible to overreact when it comes to a pandemic. I mean, I'm obviously not a doctor or anything, but if there's ever a time to overreact, it seems like it should be now?" She shrugs. "I don't think you overreacted at all. I think you just reacted. No 'over' about it."

I smile. I feel guilty for saying something a little mean, but also, gosh, it's nice to talk to someone besides my mom, who thinks this is all just the worst.

"Anyway, I guess my new question should be, on a scale of terrible to completely terrible, how terrible are you?" she asks, smiling.

I laugh. "I think right now I'm somewhere in the middle. Just medium terrible. What about you?"

"I think I'm about the same. I've been more terrible, and I've been less terrible. This seems like a medium terrible. The word *terrible* really sounds funny after a while. That's like a thing, right?"

"What's a thing? Can you be a little more specific?" I tease.

She smirks at me. "You know, when you say a word a whole bunch of times and it starts to sound funny after a while?"

My face must look completely blank, because she laughs, says, "I swear it's a thing!"

I smile at her again. "I'll take your word for it."

"I'll ask my mom next time I talk to her. That's totally something she would know."

She looks at me across the screen, and then she looks up, and then I look up, at my window, and Sadie is standing by her window. Her arm is up, leaning against the window, and since the light is on in the room behind her, she's perfectly silhouetted in the window. She looks like a painting.

"How is your mom?" I ask quietly, looking back at the screen.

She sighs, her eyes on the screen too. "I think she's more on the completely terrible side today."

"Oh man, I'm sorry."

"No, no need to apologize. Some days are easier for her than others, just like me, and this happens to be one of the less good ones."

I wait for her to elaborate, but when she doesn't, I carefully ask, "Have you heard any updates about when you might see her?"

Before she has time to answer, I quickly say, "I'm

sorry if that's way too nosy or way too personal. You don't have to answer or talk about it if you don't want to."

"It is neither of those things, so I'll answer your non-nosy and nonpersonal question. No updates." Sadie looks amused. "Things like social distancing are okay, but crossing state lines is strongly discouraged. Besides, even if she could come to New York, she'd need to quar-antine herself somewhere for two weeks, and I don't know where she'd do that since my aunt and uncle's apartment only has one bathroom. And the people in the apartment we were going to move into are still there because the people are still living in the apartment they were going to move into. It's like the worst game of dom-inoes ever."

"Right." I want to say more, but I'm afraid of making her upset.

"You look like you want to say something else," she says.

"I do," I admit. "I just don't want to make you cry."

She smiles. "I am pretty good at crying these days, I'll give you that."

"I'm just . . . I guess I'm just sorry about everything. That you can't see your mom. I don't know what I'd do if I couldn't see mine for that long. I wish . . . I wish I could do something to help. To make it better."

Sadie is quiet as she looks at me for a minute. I worry that maybe the call has frozen. Then she says, "Oh, but you are, Clarissa. You are."

I want to ask her what she means, but then she leans forward, closer toward the camera. "What's that?"

"What's what?" I try to follow her eyes, figure out what she's looking at.

"That," she says, pointing toward my desk. "Are those sketchbooks?"

I gulp. "Um, yeah, they are."

"Cool," she says.

I figure that's the end of that part of the conversation; after all, that's about as far as I've gotten in the same conversation with most people I know. I'm trying to think of what to say, to change the subject, but then Sadie says, "Want to show me what kind of stuff you like to draw?"

"You—you want to see what I draw?"

"Sure I do," she says, looking surprised. "Only if you want to show me, though."

"Do you draw too?" I ask, trying to sound casual.

"Me? Nah, I don't have an artistic bone in my body," she says, laughing. "But my cousin is an artist."

I think about how I first wondered if Sadie went to the arts high school and that's why I didn't recognize her.

It's quiet on the call for a second.

"Um, what kind of artist is your cousin?" I finally ask, to break the silence.

"Oh, she's a painter. Lots of abstract stuff. But, um, I want to talk about you and your art, not my cousin!"

"Right," I say. This is one of those conversations that

is happening so fast, one where I feel like I can't keep up, like I'm a step behind.

"You really don't like talking about your art much, do you?" she says, laughing. "I don't want to make you uncomfortable if you don't want to show it. But I also don't want to be one of those people who only talks about themselves. I've had friends like that before."

She pauses, and I realize I should say something. "Sounds annoying."

"Annoying?" She seems surprised. "No, not annoying."

"Boring?"

She laughs. "No, not that either. I guess . . . unfair?"

"Unfair to who?"

"Well, that's a good question. I guess it depends on perspective. It's unfair to me, that I don't get to know what could potentially be a really awesome person. And it's unfair to that person, that they feel like they need to or want to hold back from me."

"Really?" I say. "But what if when you get to know the person, you realize you don't actually like them, or don't like things about them? What if you liked it better before the person told you things, opened up?"

"Well, I'd prefer that, actually knowing them, the real them, over liking someone when I don't really know the true them."

"Oh," I say quietly.

"And besides, I usually have pretty good intuition about someone, if I'll like them or not."

"But how do you know?"

"Well, I don't. It's intuition," she says, grinning.

"How do you know you can trust your intuition like that?"

"I don't ever know for sure, I guess." She looks at me over the screen, gazing into my eyes. "But so far, my intuition has yet to be wrong about someone."

My insides do something kind of squishy, and I shift around in my seat.

"Anyway, about that art!" she says—my friend says— breaking the sudden silence.

"Yes," I say, trying to focus. "My art."

"Only if you're comfortable. No pressure."

I smile. "Usually people say, 'No pressure,' when there is pressure."

"Fair point," she says, smiling back. "But I really mean it! I promise."

I study her face. Her green eyes.

Before I know what I'm doing, I walk toward my sketchbook, holding my phone, holding Sadie's face.

"Okay, I'll tell you what: I'll close my eyes until you're ready to show me something. You probably weren't expecting to like exhibit your work the last time you closed your sketchbook. I don't want to totally put you on the spot."

"Right, you only want to put me on the spot a little," I say.

She smirks, then puts her hands over her eyes. "One,

two— Wait, why am I counting like I'm playing hide-and-seek with you? Let me know when you're ready."

"Sounds good." I look at her, on the screen of my phone, her eyes covered. I look out my window, across the street, and see her there, too, her eyes covered. She's waiting for me to show her my art. This girl, who I've known for less than one week, or whatever this relationship I have with her is, who I've seen across the street for less than one week, wants to see my art. This girl, who has gotten me over my video-chat aversion, who looks for me at my window, who wants to know about my parents, who wants to know anything and everything I tell her, wants to see my art.

This friend.

"You ready?" she says, snapping me out of my trance.

"Um, just one more second," I say, flipping open my sketchbook. The very first picture is one of Sadie on her fire escape.

I look up at my phone quickly to see if Sadie saw the drawing, but she's still got her eyes covered. I flip through more pages until I get to one from a few days ago, when I found out about school. It's a picture of a girl with her head down. I'm still not sure who the girl is yet. But looking at the drawing I remember the devastation I was feeling, the panic, the anger. I remember how all-encompassing my feelings were. How all-encompassing my feelings still are, how much and how suddenly and how hard they hit, if I think about the pandemic, about lockdown, for too long.

"Are you having second thoughts about showing your stuff?" Sadie asks. "You can take it back. I mean, I'll probably make you feel like crap about it, but ya know, no biggie."

I force a laugh. "You can look."

She takes her hands off her eyes, blinks a few times. "I was in there for a while," she says, laughing. Then she leans forward, looking at my sketchbook. She stops laughing. "Are you for real?"

I know I'm not very good, but I thought maybe she'd at least fake it a little. I start to close the sketchbook, feeling like a fool, but she says, "Clarissa, you did that? It's amazing. Don't close your sketchbook!"

"What?" I must have heard her wrong. I open the book back up slowly.

"That's beautiful. Wow, I can't believe you can draw like that. Like, how does your hand connect with your brain to make those shapes, those lines?"

I feel my face starting to flush a little. "Oh, it's not really that hard."

"Not that hard!" she says. "Maybe not for you! That's why it's so good."

"If you look closely, you can see all the places I messed up," I say. "Like here, I have such a hard time with noses—"

"Dude!" Sadie interrupts. "Can you take the compliment, please?"

I feel myself flushing more. "Thank you," I say quietly, looking down.

"Hey, over here!" Sadie says. I look up, and she's waving at me. Her green eyes are sparkling. "It's amazing, truly."

"Thank you," I say again, looking into those sparkling eyes. The embarrassment I felt before is replaced by something else. Something like ... gratitude. "I mean, thank you for the compliment, and thank you for asking to see it too. And I guess thank you for being a ..." I trail off, looking into her eyes.

"Hey, don't mention it," she says softly. She lifts her hand, almost like she wants to touch my face, her screen, then puts her hand back down.

She clears her throat. "Anyway! Thanks for doing that. Showing the art. Opening yourself up. I get the sense that isn't always easy for you."

"What makes you say that?" I say, surprised that she noticed.

"Well, it wasn't rocket science. I saw how squirmy you were the other night."

"I was." My own honesty surprises me. "But like I said, once I started talking more, it felt easier. It's ... it's really easy to talk to you."

I can't believe I just said that out loud. I close my eyes, mentally kicking myself, thinking she's going to think I'm some kind of weirdo, but when I open my eyes again, she doesn't even look fazed.

"Like I said, I know I'm a lot sometimes. So, thanks. For giving me your number and being my pal through all of this."

Pal.

"It's no problem," I answer honestly.

She smiles at me again, that big smile, her green eyes sparkling. She tells me about a horror movie she just watched, and I tell her about the last movie I saw in a theater.

We talk for almost two hours again. About vacations we've taken (her, all over the world; me, all over New York State and New England), about our favorite foods to eat at carnivals (her, fried anything; me, corn on the cob), about whether we like dogs or cats better (her, dogs; me, cats).

When we finally hang up, I just sit on my bed, once again wondering if it was all a dream. Wondering once again what I've started. Wondering if I should stop it.

Likes: 10,109

Comments: 2,578

23

After I talk to Sadie, I get ready for bed. I don't check Babble.

But I can't fall asleep. Again. Every time I start to doze off, a Babble comment will pop into my head, strangers asking me to prove that I'm real with a picture; Sadie will pop into my head, the way she doesn't know about the posts; Vanessa will pop into my head. Vanessa and our potential date—the date I still haven't talked to my parents about. Vanessa and college—the research I still haven't done. The money I still don't know if we will have.

When I finally, finally fall asleep, the bits of sleep I get are filled with dreams and nightmares. In one, I'm running after Vanessa on my street. There aren't any cars or people, just Vanessa and me, but I can't catch up with her. I finally get close to her, but when I reach for her hand, it turns to smoke, and then all of her turns to smoke, and she disappears.

I wake up around 5:30 and reach for my phone. I scroll through social media, but it's just a bunch of people taking selfies in their masks. Too depressing. Finally, curiosity gets the best of me, and I start reading comments from my latest post.

Yay! Finally a longer post!

Another sweet video chat!

Maybe not as romantic as the last one?

I mean, how romantic can video calls really be?

I dunno, I think they need to take their relationship to the next level.

Um, next level? Remember that whole pandemic thing?

What if they go on a socially distant date?

Yeah if they wear masks they could totally see each other.

Oh mannn you were close to getting busted! She almost saw the picture you drew of her!

Awww, you showed her your art! I don't show anyone my art.

Still waiting for you to prove that you're real, Clarissa.

Here we go again.

I smell something fishy.

Stilllll waiting for that picture!

Even more people after that comment, saying they want photographic proof, saying they think the story is fake. That I'm fake. I could just put an end to this all now, confess everything. Say it started because I saw Sadie on her fire escape, and it was just a silly little writing exercise, a way to keep my mind off the virus, a way to make myself feel better, and the posts just got out of hand. The comments, the requests, have gotten out of hand.

I love Vanessa. And would never do anything to mess that up. I could explain everything now in a post. Vanessa knows about the Babble posts. She could know the truth, that I'm the one writing them, in a matter of minutes. But I just don't feel ready.

Maybe because I've never shown Vanessa my drawings. I mean, she's caught me doodling in my notes for school, and she's seen my closed sketchbooks in my room, but she's never asked to see my drawings. I've also never offered to show them to her. But it just seems like it'd be . . . weird. Yeah, she's my girlfriend of more than six months, but my drawings are really personal, and it just seems like it'd be like offering up my heart for her to judge. And also, I guess more importantly, I figured if she really wanted to see my art, she would have asked by now? Or would have tried to look in my sketchbooks somehow. But she's just so darn respectful. Like, she'd never go behind my back to do anything, would never open my sketchbooks if I weren't in the room with her, would never open or touch something on my desk without asking first.

Next time I talk to her, I will bring up my art. Or figure out a way to get her to ask me about it. I will. I could text her or call her now, but it's still so early.

I rub my head. Still, I need to do something. I skim the comments again. What if I just do this one silly thing? Take a picture. Prove that I'm real. Just this one silly thing, and then people will believe me, and then I can stop the posts. Because I suddenly realize that I can't stop now, before I post a picture. I can't let people think I stopped the posts because I'm not real. Because Sadie isn't real. I don't know why this feels like the right course of action, why I care what a bunch of strangers think, but I also know I don't have any more time to analyze any of this, and I have to do something. Now.

I look around my room, then dig through my closet. I find an old beach hat that used to be my mom's and stick it on my head. I find an old bandanna in my closet, too, fold it a few times, and put it over the bottom part of my face like a mask. Pretty much only my eyes are sticking out now. I pull out a piece of paper, and on the paper, I scrawl, *Hi, world! I'm Clarissa*. I make my handwriting a little different than usual. I hold up the paper next to my face and take some selfies. I change the filters on my phone so my eyes look darker, almost brown, instead of my usual hazel.

It actually really looks . . . nothing like me. I take a deep breath and then post the picture.

Then I power down my laptop, put my phone in airplane mode, and go back to bed.

24

I jolt awake. I can't tell if I've been asleep for two minutes, two seconds, or two hours. I rub my eyes and turn the alerts on my phone back on. I take a deep breath, then start reading the comments on my latest Babble post.

Ahh, at long last we meet Clarissa.

You guys seriously think this is legit?

Why is she in disguise?

Could still totally be some old dude creeper in the middle of nowhere.

Okay, so even if this really is Clarissa, how do we know Clarissa is in NYC?

Wait, so Sadie doesn't even know about these posts?!

I was gonna say, we should see a picture of Sadie so we know she's real, but that'd be real creepy if she doesn't even know about these posts!

I dunno, I just want to read more about their video calls.

They should totes go on a date.

They're just friends, remember. /sarcasm

Umm, fake news, anyone?

I feel annoyed all over again. Annoyed that these Internet strangers aren't satisfied with what I gave them, annoyed that I know that they're right. Annoyed that I'm letting them get to me, and especially annoyed that I gave in to their requests. I should have just stopped with the post before. Who cares what these people think? I was hoping posting the photo would fix things somehow, that I could safely disappear back into the ether of the Internet after I put it up, but it's just made things even worse.

I don't know how to fix any of this. I do know that if I don't post again, I'll just prove all the commenters' point—that Clarissa is a big fake. That I'm a big fake. Since when did telling the truth become so hard for me?

Worst of all, I keep thinking of Sadie. What she would do if she knew about my Babble account. If she read the posts. How creepy and weird she'd think I was. How dishonest she'd think I was. How fake.

And my girlfriend. Oh my god. My girlfriend. My smart, pretty, nice girlfriend. What would she think about it all, do about it all, if she knew I was the one writing the fire escape girl posts? I feel like my throat is closing in, like I have to swallow a bunch before I can breathe normally again.

My phone keeps vibrating with new emails—people commenting on my photo post. I just feel more and more annoyed with all the comments I read. People doubting that Clarissa is real, that Sadie is real, that I'm not some old person nowhere close to New York City.

And the reason I feel most annoyed? I know they are totally right. They have no reason to believe that I am who I say I am.

I pick up the book next to my bed and start reading. Time to escape into the safety of another world again.

A little later, I go out to the kitchen to look for something to eat. It's been a while since we've gotten a grocery delivery, so our cabinets and refrigerator are looking a little bare. I grab a piece of cheese, some stale-ish crackers, and some chocolate chips I find in the back of the cabinet. While I'm dumping the chocolate chips into a cup, my mom walks into the apartment, holding a stack of envelopes. "You got some mail, honey!"

"Really?" I never get mail.

"It might have come a few days ago. You know I haven't been checking the mail right away, to cut down on germs. Anyway, looks like it's from Vanessa."

My mask! I'd almost forgotten about it.

"Melissa, stop being nosy," my dad says from the couch.

"I'm not being nosy!" my mom says. "I'm just thinking maybe I should open the envelope first?"

My dad looks up. "Give your daughter some privacy!"

"Joe, I am not being nosy," she says in a calm voice, but in one that I know is one step away from yelling. "We still don't know that the virus can't live in the mail."

"I keep telling you that's not true," my dad says.

"Oh, really, Joe, and where do you keep hearing that?"

"I didn't hear it anywhere. It's just not true."

"According to who? You? You with your doctorate in pandemics?" my mom says, her voice tight.

"Um, guys?" I wonder if they've forgotten I'm here.

My mom turns to me. "Sorry, Claire. I'm just going to open the envelope. I won't look at what's inside. I'll wash my hands now, then open the envelope, then wash them again, then hand you what's inside."

My dad starts to say something, thinks about it, and closes his mouth again.

My mom washes her hands, then slits open the envelope carefully, using only one finger. She taps the mask onto the kitchen counter with her head up, not looking at it. "Did I get whatever was inside of the envelope out, Claire?"

"Yeah, Mom."

Then she washes her hands again, keeping her eyes averted from the mask the whole time. "There you go, honey."

My dad and I watch the whole spectacle. I still can't believe how complicated getting and receiving mail has become.

"Thank you, Mom."

I scoop the mask up, then take it to my room.

I hold it in my fingers. Vanessa's fingers were on the mask, just a few days ago. I picture her sitting at the sewing machine. She feels so close and so far away from me.

I lift up the mask, hold it over my nose and mouth, put the straps over my ears. I feel the mask, then realize I have it on upside down. I flip it around, pinch the nose part to make it tighter, and look in the mirror.

I look at myself, at the mask. Vanessa really did an amazing job on it. It's so much more comfortable than the paper ones I wear when I go for quick walks with my mom. I smile at myself, remember I can't see my mouth.

There is a knock on my door. "Laundry, honey," my mom says. "Some of your pants got mixed up with mine."

"Thanks," I say, opening the door.

My mom looks at me, makes a surprised face. "What is that?"

"It's a homemade face mask. Our governor is mandating that we wear masks if we go out in public," I say sarcastically, then take off the mask.

"Ha ha, very funny. You've been spending too much time around your dad. I meant where did it come from?"

"Vanessa made it for me," I say. "It's the mail I just got."

"She made that? Wow! Is there anything that girl can't do?"

"You're telling me," I say quietly.

She either doesn't hear what I say or doesn't know how to respond, but then she says, "Wait, so why did she make you one?"

It's now or never. I take a deep breath and say, "Well, Vanessa and I were talking, thinking maybe we could see each other in person. We could—"

"Absolutely not," my mom interrupts.

"Can I finish?" I say calmly.

She nods, gestures for me to continue.

"Anyway, Vanessa and I would social distance—stay six feet apart from each other, no touching. We'd wear masks."

My mom studies my face. "So that's why you were asking about social distancing the other day. I knew something was up then."

"Yeah," I admit.

She shakes her head. "I'm sorry. My answer is no."

"Mom, come on," I protest.

"Come on what? Let you go out in the middle of a pandemic with your girlfriend? No, honey."

"But—"

"But nothing; my answer is no," she says, crossing her arms over her chest.

I expected this. But that still doesn't make it any less frustrating. I sigh loudly.

"It's just not a good idea," my mom says.

"What's not a good idea?" my dad asks, suddenly appearing next to my mom.

Do they have some kind of infrared invisible communication system or something?

"Claire wants to see Vanessa," she says.

My dad looks confused, so I chime in. "Vanessa and I were thinking we could finally have a little date. No touching, or even getting close to each other, and we'll wear masks the whole time." I hold up the mask. "See, look, a mask."

He says, "Did Vanessa get that for you?"

"Joe, Vanessa *made* it," my mom says.

"What? No way!" he responds. "Can I see it?"

I hand it over to him. He starts to put it up to his face, and I say, "Don't put that on!" at the same time my mom says, "Get that away from your face!"

He looks insulted. "I wasn't going to actually put it on, jeez. Don't know what difference it makes. In case you forgot, we've been in lockdown together anyway."

I grab the mask back from my dad. "Just—don't!" I snap.

"Anyway, Joe, focus. Your daughter wants to see her girlfriend in the middle of a pandemic. How do you feel about that?" My mom's eyes bore into his eyes. "I don't like it."

My dad looks right back at her, then at me. He sighs. "Melissa, she needs to live her life."

"Joe, it's a pandemic!"

"I'll wear my mask. Vanessa and I won't get close to each other,"

I repeat. "She's been home. Her family has been home."

"I know. I trust her. I trust you," my mom says. "It's the other people I wouldn't trust. You and Vanessa haven't seen each other in so long, and I know you'll be distracted, and you might not be paying attention and not see someone if they're not wearing a mask. And what if they're sick?"

"Mom, I'd see someone like that. And then I'd move out of the way."

"But what if *they* don't move? Or what if they know they're sick and they go out without a mask and intentionally spread their germs, trying to get other people sick?"

"Is that really a thing?" my dad asks.

"I'm sure it is!" my mom says. "People have gone crazy from being inside for so long, not living their normal lives for so long. Who knows what we're all capable of anymore."

My dad says, "And I think people are going to go even crazier if they can't have any human interaction besides over video screens or with the people they live with. Which, in our poor daughter's case, is us. Melissa, just think about it. She's been stuck with *us* for over a month straight."

"I know, but—" my mom says.

"Us," my dad says again, pointing at himself and my mom. "And they would be taking all the precautions."

My mom sighs, then turns her attention to me. "You're seventeen, almost a senior in high school, almost legally an adult."

"Soooo . . ." I say carefully, thinking maybe this conversation is going in the right direction.

"I see your point, but I still can't let you do it," my mom says. "I'm sorry."

"Are you serious?" I say, my voice shaking. I feel tears forming in my eyes, but I angrily brush them away.

"I'm really sorry, Claire. I also wish you would have asked us directly. I always tell you, you can talk to us about anything."

"I know, I'm sorry," I say. "I was just so afraid you were immediately going to say no that I didn't even want to bring it up. I guess I was looking for the right way to ask and never came up with it."

"I mean, getting a mask in the mail is one way to do it," my mom says snippily.

My dad starts to say, "Melissa, maybe you should—"

"Do not tell me to calm down!" my mom snaps.

I laugh nervously. "Yeah. It's creative, right?"

My mom smiles at me for a split second, and then I see her taking deep breaths.

"Um, no offense, but I think your reaction to Claire receiving a mask in the mail is exactly why she didn't ask you sooner," my dad says with a nervous smile.

My mom spins around to face him, and his smile is instantly gone.

"Just a hypothesis!" he says quickly, his hands up.

My mom turns to face me again. She takes another deep breath, closes her eyes for a second, then says more quietly, "I'm sorry, Claire. I wish it were something I felt comfortable with. My answer is no."

"Seriously?" I explode with anger I didn't know I had in me. "This is so unfair! Vanessa's parents are totally cool with it."

"I understand that," my mom says calmly, rubbing her head. "But I'm not Vanessa's parents. I'm your parents. Your parent. This isn't an easy decision to make. I just don't feel comfortable with it."

My dad looks back and forth between my mom and me, like he's watching a tennis match. "Maybe we should all try to calm down?"

My mom and I both whirl to look at him at the same time. He jumps.

"Just an idea!" he says quickly.

"Well, it's too late, anyway!" I yell angrily. "Thanks for nothing, both of you."

I slam the door in both of their faces, wiping my angry tears away.

I hear my parents whispering outside my door, but I just put on music so I don't have to listen to them. Though my crying drowns them out too.

I pace my room, wiping at my face.

When will I be able to see my girlfriend again in person, not over a screen? Kiss my girlfriend again? Hold her hand? Go to the movies with her again? Will any of this ever end? I hate how mad I am at my parents right now. I hate all of this.

I look at myself in my mirror again, put my mask on again, wiping my tears away. My eyes are puffy and red, but at least the mask hides my tearstained cheeks. I snap a selfie, send it to Vanessa.

Claire:

Thank you.

Vanessa:

You're welcome! Looks so good on you, babe!

I realize it's the first time I've been complimented about the mask I'm wearing, which makes me cry again.

Vanessa:

Please tell me you talked to your parents!

Claire:

I did.

That part is true, at least. And that part feels almost good, telling the truth about something. Something.

Vanessa:

Claire:

Um, not so yay, actually.

Vanessa:

Whaaaat? Please tell me you're kidding.

Claire:

Not kidding.

Vanessa:

Oh, babe, this stinks. Maybe my mom can talk to your mom?

I think about it for a second. About Vanessa's mom trying to talk my mom into something, and it is tempting, but it also just feels . . . icky in some way I can't put my finger on.

Claire:

Oh, maybe.

Vanessa:

Why didn't they say yes?

Claire:

Because we want to see each other in the middle of a pandemic?

I realize it's a little snippy, but she's making me feel crummy. And I'm still mad at my parents, but I feel like she's implying my parents are being ignorant, my mom is being ignorant.

Vanessa:

Ouch!

Claire:

Sorry.

Vanessa:

Well, if your mom wants to talk to my mom or anything, maybe they could talk later today? My mom works long hours, but she's free later tonight.

Claire:

So does mine.

I add the smiley face at the last second to disguise my annoyance. My mom is just as hard of a worker as Vanessa's mom.

Vanessa:

This is a drag, but we'll figure something out, okay? About to make scones! Talk after?

Was also thinking about our next movie night. There's that documentary about penguins we could watch.

Claire:

Okay.

The last thing I feel like doing is thinking about our next video-chat movie night. But I don't know how to tell Vanessa that.

Vanessa:

Cool, will call you later?

Claire:

You got it.

I try to read my book, but I'm still too upset to focus. I can't believe how unreasonable my parents are being. I can't believe I don't know when I can see my girlfriend again. Touch my girlfriend again.

I think about my creative writing teacher telling us that writing can be therapeutic. A way to release emotions.

I open my laptop. I don't owe anyone on Babble anything, but I'm allowed to talk about my emotions and feelings on my own Babble account. So that's exactly what I'm going to do.

25

I got in a fight with my parents today. We never used to fight. We never used to do a lot of the things we've been doing lately. It makes me feel so . . . sad.

And when I'm feeling sad, I talk to my friends to make me feel better. My friends. My friend Sadie. I text her.

> Clarissa:
> What are you up to?

Sadie:
Having a big party.
Might watch a movie.

> Clarissa:
> Oh yeah? What kind?

I'm just making conversation with her, I'm not trying to—

Sadie:
A scary one. Want to watch with me?

Oh god, that was definitely not what I was trying to do, to get her to watch a movie with me.

Clarissa:
Maybe.
Maybe we could just video-chat for now?

Sadie:
You know I'm down! I was going to ask but thought you might be busy.

I don't write anything back, and then my phone vibrates with a call.

Sadie.

I answer it, and there she is. Green eyes sparkling, that smile lighting up my phone screen.

Her smile fades a little when she looks at me. I must look worse than I thought.

"Trouble in paradise?" she asks. I try to smile, and she quickly says, "You don't have to talk about it if you don't want to. Whatever 'it' is. Or maybe there isn't even an 'it.' Maybe you just feel regular terrible or totally terrible because of that whole pandemic thing. Which I'm happy to either talk to you about or not talk to you about. Ya know."

I can't help but smile, listening to her, watching her.

"You ever been really disappointed about something that feels like the worst kind of disappointment ever?" I blurt out.

"No," she says quickly, not missing a beat.

"Gee, thanks, that's making me feel so much better," I say, but I'm still smiling.

"Well, you didn't tell me that I was supposed to tell you something to make you feel better. When someone asks a question, I like to answer truthfully." She smiles back at me.

"So if I asked you if you liked one of my outfits and you didn't, you'd tell me?"

"I mean, sure, but why does what I think about one of your outfits matter?"

I sigh. She's too good at this. "Fine, what if . . . what if I asked if you thought I was pretty, and you didn't think so, would you tell me?" The words fly out of my mouth before I can stop them. I rub my eyes. There's no way I can look her in the face now.

"Well, I'd never go out of my way to tell someone I didn't find them attractive. I mean, what's the point of that? Everyone has different tastes in everything—food, people, clothes, whatever. It's not like I go around point-ing at what people are eating at restaurants, saying 'Ewww, I'd never eat that!' And anyway, all people are beautiful in their own way."

She says it so simply, I feel silly for getting embar-rassed. I'm ready to change the subject, or at least go back to my original question, but Sadie quickly says, "But, if you must know, you're beautiful."

I inhale sharply, look back at the screen, and Sadie is

looking right into my eyes. I pull my eyes away from the screen, look up, across the street, and I see Sadie in her window looking right at me there too.

She clears her throat, and I look back at my screen again. "Anyway, I feel like you had a question, about being disappointed?"

"Right," I say quickly, shaking my head.

"Like I said before, I usually make a habit of getting to know someone, like maybe asking too many personal questions. But doing that prevents me from finding out I don't really know someone down the line, and leading to them disappointing me, or doing something to disappoint me. But I also realize not everyone operates that way," she says.

I smile at her. I can't help it. I've never met anyone who thinks the way she does, acts the way she does.

"I'm assuming you don't operate that way? And now someone has done something to disappoint you, and you've gotten a different outcome than what you were expecting? I'm just going out on a limb here," she says, shrugging.

I laugh. "Yeah, okay, you nailed it."

She laughs back. Gosh, that little chipped tooth in the front of her mouth. I wonder if she feels it push against her lips. Her lips . . . I watch them move, then realize she's asked me a question.

"Oh, um, sorry, you froze for a second," I say.

"Oh, weird, you didn't," she says, maybe a little

suspiciously. "So do you want to tell me about this disappointing person in your life?"

"I'm not sure yet," I say honestly. I don't know if I can accurately sum up how confused I feel about my friendships, my relationships, right now.

I worry I've hurt Sadie's feelings, but she says, "That's cool. Well, you know where to find me."

I grin.

She grins back. It's quiet for a second, us looking at each other across our screens. Finally, she says, "So, you don't like scary movies or horror movies?"

"Not really?" I say.

"I get it; they're not everyone's cup of tea."

"I guess I feel like if I'm going to invest an hour and a half or two hours of my life into something, I'd rather it be funny?"

"Oh, but that's where you are wrong! Some scary movies are the funniest things I've ever seen," she says.

"Really?" I ask skeptically.

"Totally!"

"Do you have a super-twisted sense of humor or something?" I ask, wondering if I've been judging her wrong all along.

"I mean, possibly, but I don't think you have to have a weird sense of humor to think horror movies are funny."

"That sounds like something someone with a twisted sense of humor would say. Rationalizing."

"Hmm, fair point, fair point. Well, you let me know

when you're ready to be indoctrinated into the world of comedy horror, and I will drop whatever it is I'm doing."

"Deal," I say.

"I don't exclusively watch horror movies either, by the way. Like, I'm open to trying new kinds of movies," she says.

I wonder where she's going with this, and then she says, "And my calendar right now is pretty open. If you were going to watch a movie. If you felt like watching a movie together. I've done it with a few of my friends back home. Some don't like it. Which I realize you might be one of them. Considering how video-chat averse you were at first."

"You're not ever going to let me live that down, are you?" I ask, smiling.

"I'd say there is a decent chance of that." She's smiling right back at me. "So, what's the verdict? Movie, yea or nay?"

"Um . . ." I look into her green eyes. "Yea."

"Now I'm going to say yay. Yay!" Sadie says.

I laugh.

"So what are we going to watch?" she asks eagerly.

"Wait, you want me to pick?"

"Um, I believe that was part of the original agreement," she says. She tries to keep a straight face, but we both end up laughing.

I don't know why, but I feel like I might be blushing.

I scroll through the video services on my laptop. "How about *Everything, Everything*?" I say.

"I know nothing about it," Sadie says. "Perfect!"

"Wait, seriously?" I say, shocked.

"Nada," she says.

I swallow my shock. "Um, it's based on a young adult novel, and the main character can't go outside. It's such a good book!"

I don't usually talk about my favorite books, but I really can't believe she's never heard of it.

"So timely!" Sadie says. "Let's do it."

So we watch *Everything, Everything*. I'm not sure what I was expecting, watching a movie with her, but it's completely different than watching a movie with other people. Sadie yells, "Pause" when she has a question or wants to say something, so the actual movie-watching part is really quiet. Like, I've seen the movie a bunch of times already, but I'm actually able to watch the whole thing again.

The movie is a little over ninety minutes, but with all the pausing we do, it takes us over two hours to get through it. I don't mind at all.

When we're watching the end credits, Sadie yells, "Pause!" again.

I look at her, waiting for her question or comment or observation, but she just looks back at me. "You said 'Pause,' right?" I ask.

"Yes, I did. I realized I wanted to say something but

didn't actually figure out what I wanted to say ahead of time."

"You think before you speak?" I tease.

She smirks at me. "Believe it or not, sometimes I do."

It's weird, I can like actually see her thinking. Finally, she says, "Just, thanks, I guess, is all."

"It took you that long to figure out what you wanted to say, and that was it? I was hoping you were going to tell me your theories on quantum physics." I can't help but grin at her.

She grins back, says, "Sometimes saying less is saying more."

"Did you read that on a fortune cookie?"

She grins again, then yawns. It's getting late. "I think I might actually be tired."

Watching her yawn makes me realize I'm tired too. "Same here."

"I'm going to go, then, before I fall asleep while we're still on the call," she says, with another big yawn. "Good night."

"Good night."

She looks at me one more time before she disconnects the call.

It's not until she's hung up that I realize I still don't know what she was thanking me for.

26

The next day after school, I've got my trigonometry textbook open in front of me, Vanessa on a video chat, but once again I can't focus on my homework. My mind keeps wandering to Babble. I was only able to read through a handful of the comments from my latest posts just before I started my homework with Vanessa.

> Movie over video chat, duh! I gotta try that.
>
> She called her beautiful!
>
> Um so obvs Sadie likes her!
>
> And obvs Clarissa likes her!
>
> This is all a deflection for Clarissa posting such an unhelpful picture!
>
> So wait, why is Clarissa fighting with her parents?
>
> And what is she so disappointed about?

Or who is she so disappointed about?

That was some major vague-posting.

That picture did literally nothing to prove that she's real.

I wish they'd just meet up already! This is cute and all, but I feel like they need to see each other closer up.

Mask up and go out!

Only a few people seemed satisfied with my picture, and now it seems like people aren't satisfied with what I'm writing either. My writing. These people were so excited about and interested in the posts at first, and now all they want to do is criticize me. These strangers. They just ask more of me, more from me, more about me, tell me what I should write, what I shouldn't write, what I should do, what I shouldn't do. With each new post that I write, I keep hoping it will answer people's questions, satisfy them, but it seems like each post just leads to more questions, more requests.

The Internet is supposed to be a place for people to distract themselves from their problems, from thinking about things like the virus, their real life, and it seems like these posts are just creating more problems, more things for me to worry about. Because now it's all following me into my non-Internet life too.

I don't know how to fix any of this.

"Are you okay?" Vanessa asks. I'm startled to look back at the screen and see that she's staring at me.

"Yeah, I'm fine," I say automatically.

Then I think about how comfortable conversations with Sadie are, how easy it was to open up to her. Maybe I've been hiding too much of myself from Vanessa.

"You don't think this is all super depressing?" I blurt out.

Vanessa looks surprised. "What's depressing? How much homework we have? I mean, yeah, I guess it is a little, but I don't think our teachers are being unfair or anything with how much they're giving us."

"What? No, I'm not talking about homework." I can feel my frustration building.

Vanessa looks at me, waiting for me to go on.

"Not homework," I say. "Quarantine. Lockdown. Whatever. Not being able to see each other. Touch each other. Remember when we used to do homework together in person? Remember when we could sit next to each other to watch a movie?"

Vanessa sighs. "Claire, I don't know what you want me to say. We've already talked about this. It's not my fault we can't see each other!"

"I know, I know," I say. I hear the impatience and snippiness in my own voice, but I'm not sure if Vanessa does.

"And yeah, it stinks, like a lot, but just think big picture; we're very fortunate."

"Yeah, I know, we're healthy, we're young."

"Also, we're in one of the biggest cities in the world. Like, there is no shortage of people out there who can make our lives easier," she continues.

"Easier? You think this is a good time to think about how our lives can be easier?" I have a sudden weird feeling about where this conversation is headed.

"I just meant we have a lot of resources available. Lots of things are really accessible to us. Things we wouldn't have if we lived somewhere else."

"What kind of resources?" I say slowly.

"Well, food delivery services, delivery people."

"Wait, are you seriously calling human beings 'resources'?" I ask, my frustration going from a low simmer to a boiling rage.

She sighs again. "Okay, that came out wrong. I just meant, we have all these people working, people willing to make our lives easier."

"Um, I was kinda thinking this is a good time to think about how we can make other people's lives less hard."

"Right," Vanessa says impatiently. "And one way we can make other people's lives less hard is by providing them with an income."

"You really think a pandemic is the best time to be ordering delivery?"

"Claire, what else are we supposed to do? Let these businesses go bankrupt?" she snaps.

"I can't believe you called people 'resources'!" I sputter.

"It was the wrong choice of words. I'm working on my economics homework. My mind is on numbers. I'm sorry."

I look at her, wondering how I'm just now seeing this side of her. "I thought you and your family were cooking a bunch, baking, trying new recipes. Have you been ordering delivery?" I try not to roll my eyes, but I'm not sure if I'm successful.

"Well, I mean, not at all the recipes always work out, and sometimes my parents want better coffee than the stuff in their coffee maker, and—"

"The recipes don't work out?! You always talk about how good all the stuff is that you guys make! You send me pictures!"

She shrugs. "Okay, maybe sometimes I overhype some of it a bit. And maybe sometimes some of it looks better in a picture with a bunch of filters added than it actually tastes."

I'm trying to digest everything she's telling me, but I keep coming back to something. "So you've been ordering delivery?"

Now she rolls her eyes. "I mean, yeah, just a little here and there. Nowhere close to how much we used to order or anything, just maybe a few times a week. It's not that big of a deal."

"Not that big of a deal?" I sputter. "You've been lying to me!"

"Lying? Are you for real?" Vanessa looks shocked.

"Uh, yeah, you've been sending me pictures of your food, telling me about your food, and you've never mentioned delivery!"

"Babe, chill! I never said we weren't getting delivery. That would be a lie. All these studies are saying the virus can't be passed through food anyway. I don't know why you're getting so worked up. I didn't lie about anything. I'm not putting anyone in any danger."

I think about her great-aunt, who I didn't even know about, who just died, and now this.

"It just seems a little . . . something. I don't know, ordering food, making people make you food—"

"A little what?" Vanessa interrupts. "What were you going to say, Claire? Go ahead, spit it out."

"Fine!" I snap. "It's a little selfish, don't you think? If you're so concerned about these 'resources,' your parents could always make a donation to the restaurants instead?"

"That's so insulting!"

"*Insulting?*" I practically yell. "You're the one who called them 'resources'!"

"And I said I was sorry. I said the wrong word. I don't know what else you want me to say," Vanessa says patiently, rubbing her head.

"I think I need to go."

"I think that's a good idea."

The truth is, I want her to stop me, to say she's sorry for making me think she's someone she's not, for lying about things, for not being up front about things. And then maybe I can tell her I'm writing the fire escape girl posts, that I've been lying too, and we can both be sorry and stop fighting so much. But she quickly leans over and disconnects the call.

I stare at my laptop, at my screen.

Then I sigh. I can't believe she called people *resources*. I can't believe she's been ordering delivery. Now my mom seems a little less unreasonable for not wanting me to see Vanessa. And I really can't believe how much we've been arguing these last few days.

I open up Babble without even realizing what I'm doing, and it's just more people commenting, people who don't believe I am who I say I am, people speculating whether or not Clarissa and Sadie like each other, people planning a date, people saying my last post was boring, and it's just too much.

These posts, silly updates, were supposed to be a distraction, a way for me to feel better, maybe a little less scared, a little less hopeless. And they're not. Nothing is making me feel any better about anything. I don't know if anything is ever going to make me feel good again. I can't imagine feeling anything other than annoyance, anger, frustration, and a lack of hope.

The lack of hope scares me the most.

I think about texting Vanessa, telling her I'm sorry, but I'm way too mad about her use of the word *resources*. About her ordering delivery. And thinking about all that makes me mad all over again, that now I'm judging someone for ordering delivery. This is what things have come to? I now judge people, judge my girlfriend, for ordering delivery?

I pace around my room, trying to figure out what to do. About my Babble posts. With the rest of my day. I guess I'll finally have some coveted alone time. I really need to be more careful about what I wish for.

And I'm also aware that the number of notifications on my phone is going up, so it doesn't really feel like time to myself when so many people, so many strangers, have the ability to affect my mood.

Maybe I'll watch another movie. That was actually a good distraction last night. A movie Vanessa would never watch with me. She's pretty particular about what she'll watch. Maybe I'll watch a scary movie?

27

Posted by Clarissareads:

I'm talking to Sadie on a video call. We've just realized we can't remember the last birthday we blew out candles on a cake, and we don't know when or if we can ever do it again. It's horrible and depressing, but we're both laughing.

Sadie says between tears of laughter, "Gosh, pandemics are such a drag."

And then we both start laughing even harder.

"Hey, I know I keep harping on the horror movies thing—"

"You like horror movies?" I interrupt. "I hadn't heard."

She smirks at me over the screen. "Anyway, before someone interrupted me—"

"Who would do that? So rude! You should really tell that person to stop."

She narrows her eyes at me and tries to look mad, but then smiles again. "I'm going to watch a horror movie. Do you want to watch one with me? It might be a good distraction. If you want. Maybe. I don't know. Unless you don't want to, since we just watched a movie last night. And I know you probably have things to do."

"I'd love to," I say.

"Really?" Sadie looks surprised.

"Really."

"Ohhh, what to watch, what to watch," she says, steepling her fingers together under her chin. Her eyes light up. "I have just the thing!"

"Oh yeah?"

"Yes! Look up *The Village*."

"Wait a second," I say, suddenly thinking of something. "This isn't some kind of pandemic end-of-the-world horror movie, right? I think that might just hit a little too close to home. I mean, I know I picked a movie about not being able to go outside yesterday, but at least it had a happy ending!"

"What kind of monster do you think I am?" Sadie asks, her eyes wide.

"I don't know!" I say quickly. "I just wanted to make sure!"

Sadie smiles, then gives a little evil laugh. "Just trust me, Clarissa."

I look into her eyes, and horror movie or not, I do.

I open up my streaming movies on my laptop, find *The Village*, and look at Sadie.

"Okay, you ready for this?" she asks with a gleam in her eye.

"As ready as I'll ever be, I guess," I say apprehensively.

"Here we go!" We both hit play at the same time, and the movie starts.

Sadie is right about one thing—the movie is a great distraction. I'm way too focused on it to think about school or the virus or college or paying for college or fighting with my parents or anything, except where the creature in the woods is, or when it's going to make an appearance again. Sadie yells "pause" a few different times to make sure I'm okay with the movie, not too scared or anything, and I realize I'm not scared. I'm completely mesmerized.

At one particularly tense part, when the creature has been spotted, I cover my eyes. When I move my hands again, I look at my phone screen, and Sadie is watching me.

I wonder if I should yell "pause" myself, if she has something to tell me or ask me, but before I can say anything, she looks away from me and back at her laptop again.

I focus on the movie again, and once again I forget about everything except that monster in the woods.

When the credits of the movie roll, I take a deep breath. I realize it's the first deep breath I've taken since the movie started.

Sadie is watching me with an eager look on her face. "Soooo, what did you think?" she asks.

"I can't believe that ending!"

"Right? Did you like it, I mean, aside from that? Like, do you regret watching? Is it going to give you nightmares or anything? Would you watch another scary movie with me? Do you like comedies better? Is this too many questions?" She smiles.

I start laughing. "Yes, no, no, yes, I'm not sure, and probably."

She starts laughing too. "Sorry, sometimes I get a little excited."

I'm still laughing. "I hadn't noticed."

But I'm thinking about something too.

"So . . . why did you pick this movie?" I ask.

She studies me, her face suddenly serious. "I like it because things aren't always what they seem."

"Are you talking about the movie? Or in real life?" I ask carefully.

Sadie smiles, her serious look gone as quickly as it appeared. "What do you think?"

"I think that you're answering my question with a question," I say.

"Why would I do that?" She smiles innocently at me. Then she squints at something on her laptop screen. "Sorry, I just got a text from my mom."

"Is everything okay?"

"Yeah, she's just taking a break in her lesson planning."

I can hear her typing as she looks at her laptop screen. She looks back at me. "I'm sorry, I'm being so rude," she says.

"Um, she is your mom!" I say. "Don't worry about it."

"Thanks, Clarissa," she says, still looking at me.

I hear something ping on her computer, and she says, "How about I talk to you later so you don't have to watch me text with my mom?"

I want to tell her that it's okay, that watching her is no trouble, but I keep my mouth shut. "That sounds good."

"Cool," she says, smiling. "Thanks, Clarissa."

"Tell your mom I said hi," I say, and then wonder why I've said it. I've never even met her mom.

"Oh, I will," she says. "She already knows all about you."

"She does?" I try to keep my voice calm, neutral, but I'm not sure if I succeed.

"Yeah, of course," she says. Her computer pings again. "Talk soon!"

She disconnects the call, and I wonder what she's told her mom about me, and I wonder why I care.

28

I close my laptop and realize my stomach is gurgling. I've managed to avoid my parents all day, but now I'm really hungry.

I can hear the TV in the living room. Sounds like one of those home improvement channels my mom puts on and leaves on in the afternoons sometimes. She could be sitting on the couch, or she could be in her room, or the kitchen. I haven't spoken to either of my parents since our fight yesterday.

My stomach gurgles again. I sigh. I can't avoid my parents forever. Especially now, when none of us can go anywhere.

I take a deep breath, open my bedroom door, and walk down the hall to the kitchen.

The living room and kitchen are both empty.

I breathe a sigh of relief I didn't know I was holding in. I open the fridge and poke around until I find some end pieces of bread. But when I turn around, someone is right behind me. Staring at me.

Someone I don't recognize. Because their face is covered in a layer of someone else's skin. I don't realize I'm screaming until my mom comes flying out of her bedroom, and the person puts their hands up, saying, "Whoa, Claire, calm down!"

I look more closely at the person. "Dad?"

He waves and smiles.

"What the heck is all over your face?" I sputter. "It looks like you're wearing someone else's skin! And why were you just standing there staring at me?"

"I didn't want to scare you," he says in a quiet voice.

"Well, mission FAIL!" I yell, waving my arms wildly. "What *is* that on your face?"

"It's a sheet mask!" he says defensively. "It's supposed to exfoliate my skin and make me look younger."

"It does kind of make you look like a serial killer," my mom says, finally speaking. I look over at her, and even though she's talking to my dad, she's looking at me.

"Just wait until I take this thing off! You guys won't even recognize me," he says.

"Um, already been there once today, Dad," I say, looking at my mom.

My mom snickers, which makes me laugh, which makes my mom laugh more. My dad crosses his arms. "Oh, you two are so funny," he says dramatically. "Self-care is more important now than ever. Experts agree!"

"'Experts,'" my mom says, making air quotes.

"Yeah, experts in what?" I chime in.

My dad's phone alarm goes off from inside his pocket. "Ooh! Time to take it off! See you ladies later." He does finger guns at my mom and me before heading into the bathroom.

I watch him close the door, and when I turn around again, my mom is still looking at me. We just look at each other in silence.

"Has he always been such a dork?" I finally say.

My mom laughs. "Honey, he's been telling dad jokes since he learned to talk."

I shake my head.

"Listen, Claire," my mom begins. "About our conversation yesterday . . ."

And then she stops.

I look at her, waiting for her to go on.

"I'm just really sorry," she finally says. "I'm sorry I said you couldn't see Vanessa. I'm sorry things have to be so complicated. I'm sorry you are stuck at home with your dad and me. I'm sorry that you have so little space from your dad and me these days. Anyway, I want to talk to you. I hope it will make things a little better. A little more bearable."

"Did you develop a cure for the virus?"

"Don't I wish." My mom smiles sadly. "But it's related to the virus."

"A vaccine?" I smile, despite myself.

My mom smirks at me. "I think your dad and I were too hard on you."

"About?" I ask, surprised.

"Okay, *I* was too hard on you. About seeing Vanessa." She sighs. "You can see her."

"Wait, what? Are you serious?"

"Serious as a pandemic."

I cringe. "Dark much, Mom? But are you serious, I can see Vanessa? You were so against it yesterday. What happened? What changed?" My head is whirling.

"Well, your dad and I talked. We even talked to our doctor, who said that as long as you and Vanessa both wear masks and stay six feet apart, it should be okay. You know our case numbers are even going down in the city? And the testing is now done rapidly, so people get the results in the amount of time it takes to drink a glass of water."

"I thought I saw something on the news about the numbers going down and rapid testing. Or maybe online. It's so hard to keep track sometimes. Like, my eyes kinda can't focus on all the numbers and information," I say. "But wait, I can see Vanessa?!"

She laughs. "Yes. Everything people have been doing, staying inside, in lockdown, and mask wearing, it's working. It's good news. I mean, good news for a pandemic."

"Right," I say carefully. "So, I can seriously see Vanessa?"

My mom squeezes my hand. "Yes."

All of a sudden, we hear yelling from the bathroom. My mom says quietly, "How much do you want to bet he can't get the mask off?"

And I'm so excited that I can see my girlfriend, but I'm still freaked out about this pandemic, and I still don't know what to do about my Babble posts, or what I'm going to do with my life as far as college goes or paying for college goes, but I can see my girlfriend! Any anger I felt toward my mom has vanished.

"Thanks, Mom." I wrap my arms around her. She's surprised at first, then hugs me back. My dad's yells get louder.

"I guess we better help him," my mom says, her voice in my hair.

"Do we have to?"

I pull back from my mom, and we both start laughing.

My fingers buzz with excitement.

Claire:

They changed their minds! We can see each other.

Vanessa:

Babe, please tell me you're not kidding.

Claire:

I promise!

Neither one of us mentions our conversation from before, but it suddenly doesn't seem important anymore.

Vanessa:

OMG, when? Today? When? What time?

Claire:

30 seconds too soon? ☺

Vanessa:

How about in like 30 minutes?!

Claire:

Okay. That seems more reasonable.

Vanessa:

Okay, talk soon. See you soon!!!!

Claire:

Eeee!!

Vanessa:

Oh, right, what should we do? Lol. I'll come to you?

Claire:

Right. Haha. Perfect! See you soon!!!

Vanessa:

What am I supposed to do for thirty minutes?! I have more home-work, but I can't focus. Maybe, real quick, I'll just take a quick peek and see if anyone commented on the latest post yet. Just a quick peek, I tell myself, as I open the Babble app on my phone.

Getting a little bored of these movie video chats.

She still hasn't posted a better picture.

That movie is totally not scary.

I bet I've lived in New York longer than her.

That has nothing to do with anything.

I'm not sure I buy any of this.

So many haters! Can't you guys just enjoy the story?

Sadie told her mom about Clarissa!

Still don't know why Clarissa is fighting with her parents.

Or what she's disappointed about.

I still think it's sweet.

I do too! Just, do we know it's real?

Also, when is Clarissa going to tell Sadie about these posts?? If she doesn't do it soon, it's going to be a little creepy, right? I sure wouldn't like it if I found out a bunch of Babble posts were being written about me.

I scroll through the rest of the comments, and I just feel more annoyed, more angry. What is with these people? What more do they want from me? But I am not going to let these comments, these strangers, affect my date with my girlfriend. My date with my girlfriend!

Well, I'll just write a quick post, just to shut them up. Just so I can have a clear head for my date with Vanessa. My date with Vanessa!

Just a quick post first.

29

Gotta keep this short again. I'm about to go outside! So weird how it's become such a novelty. How often I used to leave my apartment and not think twice about it. I'm just about to head out, when my phone buzzes.

> Sadie:
> My friends are talking about doing socially distant hangouts. Everyone is talking about doing socially distant hangouts! Lol.

I look across the street. She wrote *lol*, and made it seem like a joke, but I have a feeling she doesn't think it's funny in the slightest. I feel so guilty that I'm getting tired of spending so much time with my parents when Sadie can't even see her own mom.

Sadie's curtain is closed, though, so I can't see her room. Can't see if she is actually laughing out loud or not.

I want to say something, but I also know there is nothing I can say to make anything any better for her.

So I don't text anything back at all.

Likes: 8,516

Comments: 1,536

30

I stand in front of my closet. Vanessa has seen me every day over video chat. And before that she'd see me every day at school, every weekend. She's pretty familiar with my unexciting wardrobe. Still, I feel like I want to wear something . . . different, or special somehow, for my date with her.

I dig through my closet. Do I pick an outfit to match the blue polka dots on my mask? Is that too matchy-matchy? Do I pick a different pattern, one to intentionally clash with the polka dots? Pick something with polka dots?

I finally settle on a pair of leggings and a purple tunic. I start to put on lip gloss, realize it's pointless, and settle on a dab of mascara. I put my hair in a low ponytail, clipping back the loose pieces. Five minutes before the agreed-upon time with Vanessa, I slip on my mask.

My mom and dad are in the kitchen, and they both stop talking when I walk into the room. I see my mom's eyes start to well up, and I warn, "Mom."

"I'm sorry, honey. It's so hard to see you in the mask, that you have to wear it to see Vanessa."

"I know, Mom."

Even my dad is quiet and looking serious for once.

My mom takes a deep breath. "Okay. You have your hand sanitizer?"

I open my tote to show her it's in there.

"And I know you haven't seen Vanessa in person in a really long time and must be dying to touch her, but remember—"

"Yes, Mom, I know. Stay six feet apart."

"Maybe *dying* isn't the best choice of words right now, Melissa?" my dad says. Then he winks at me. I roll my eyes at him, smile at my mom. Then I remember that she can't see me smile.

My mom stands up, gives me a big hug, and then my dad gets up, gives me an awkward one-armed hug that kind of turns into a pat on the back.

I release myself from them, and then I head out of the apartment. It's just like old times when I used to go out with Vanessa, or my friends. Or go anywhere, really.

Except now I'm in a mask. And I can't touch my girlfriend.

I head down the stairs to my stoop. When I get outside, I finally start to feel nervous, anxious. It's a beautiful spring evening, and the sidewalks should be packed. I should be annoyed about how packed they are, about people walking too slow, but I don't see a single person walking around. It gives me the creeps and makes me feel sad, and also makes me feel something like homesick. Is it possible to be homesick for a time period? A time when things were normal?

I feel like I'm about to cry, but I don't want to. I don't want to get my face wet, get my mask wet. And I don't want to take off my mask either. The recycled air of my apartment seems so much safer than the fresh city air right now. I try to take a deep breath, but the air gets stuck in my mask, and I start to feel a little claustrophobic. And hot. The humidity seems stronger than it did only a few seconds ago. I start to pull the mask away from my face, then remember I shouldn't touch my face. I squirt some hand sanitizer on my hands, then try to readjust my mask with the tip of one of my fingers. But it feels crooked now.

I'm poking at the mask with my finger when I see that Vanessa is across the street, right by Sadie's building. But I don't realize it's Vanessa at first because my brain isn't used to seeing my girlfriend in person anymore, and it's definitely not used to seeing my girlfriend in a mask in person.

It's not until I feel her staring at me that I realize it's her. My girlfriend. I want to hug her, kiss her, touch her, do anything, but I can't. Somehow, this might actually be worse than seeing her on a screen. I feel tears in my eyes, remind myself I don't want to get my mask wet, shouldn't get my mask wet, and then I see Vanessa wiping her own face.

She crosses the street, stops right in front of my building.

She's looking at me, but I can't see her mouth. I can't see her smile. She says something, but I can't hear her well either, because her voice is muffled behind her mask. "What did you say?" I say to her, but I can tell by the look on her face she can't understand me either.

"It's really hard to hear you!" I shout.

She nods, looking relieved, shouts back, "I didn't realize how hot these cloth masks would be!"

"Me neither," I say. I'm pretty sure she doesn't hear me, but I think we both don't want to keep saying "what."

We just stand there, looking at each other. How is that the girl who fills up my phone with texts doesn't have anything to say to me now?

As she stands there, I see the window of Sadie's apartment open. She climbs out to the fire escape, book in hand. She looks down at me, then at Vanessa.

Oh god.

I'm with Vanessa. My girlfriend. Who I've never even told Sadie about. My girlfriend. Who also doesn't know about Sadie.

But it's weird—Sadie has a completely blank look on her face. Almost like she doesn't recognize me. Or know me. It must be the mask, I tell myself.

Now that I'm looking up at her, it's like my mind can fill in the different angles and different perspectives it was lacking before. It's like seeing someone on TV or in a movie and then seeing them in person. Somehow she seems so much more real. Her face remains blank, though, as she looks down at us, no trace of recognition on her face. She opens her book, starts reading.

I pull my eyes away, realize Vanessa is watching me. She turns around, following my eyes, and looks up at Sadie.

Before she can say anything, I say loudly, "Let's go for our walk."

Vanessa turns back to me, her eyebrows raised, and says, "That's a good idea."

I get up from the stoop, start to walk down the steps, but Vanessa quickly starts backing up down the sidewalk. "Six feet!" she says.

"Oh, right, sorry," I mumble.

"What?"

"Sorry!" I say louder.

"It's okay. Which way?"

"Um, you decide." She was always in charge before lockdown; I don't see why things should be any different now.

Vanessa nods, like she was expecting me to say that, and she starts walking. I give one quick look to Sadie, who is smirking at something in her book. At least I think it's something in her book.

Vanessa has always been a fast walker, so I jog a little bit to catch up with her. Not too much, though. She strides ahead of me, and I'm six feet behind her, and I feel like a little kid trying to catch up with her mom.

"Wait, Vanessa! You're walking too fast!"

She turns around, and I think she might be smiling, but of course it's impossible to tell. "Sorry!" she says. "Habit. I've been so used to walking with my family or alone. I think I kind of forgot you were there?"

"Gee, thanks," I say, maybe a bit more snippily than I mean to.

She either doesn't hear me or doesn't want to acknowledge what I just said.

"So, where are we headed?" I ask.

"It's up to me?"

"Um, isn't that what we just said? That you'd decide?" I say, confused. Why is taking a walk with my girlfriend so hard?

"I thought you just meant I should decide which way we should turn on the sidewalk from your apartment. I didn't know I was in charge of the entire direction of our walk. Of our *date*."

"Oh," I say. "Sorry." But I'm not totally sure what I'm apologizing for.

"It's okay," she says. "Let's just go this way, anyway." Then she turns around and starts striding again.

"Vanessa, can you go a little slower?" I say, panting to keep up with her again. I feel some moisture forming under my mask, and I'm not sure if I'm sweating or if I have a runny nose. I know I can't take off my mask to find out.

She doesn't hear me, though, and turns a corner. I follow her, poking at my mask with my fingertip.

She's stopped, finally, standing in front of a boarded-up bodega. "Does this work?" she asks. "I figure a lot of people shouldn't be walking this way."

I want to tell her it absolutely doesn't, that nothing about standing six feet away from her while we're wearing masks in front of a boarded-up bodega is romantic or date-like at all, but I don't.

We just stand there, looking at each other from at least six feet apart. Someone comes around the corner, walking their dog. They see us, then cross to the other side of the street.

"What was that for?" I ask. "Hasn't that person ever seen two girls on a date before?"

"Babe, chill out. How wide do you think these sidewalks are?"

"I dunno, pretty narrow," I say. "Oh." It sinks in. "Six feet."

"Right," she says. "I didn't see a lot of people on the walk to your place, but the people I did see I either crossed the street to get away from, or they crossed the street to get away from me."

"That's so weird," I say. We're quiet again. I finally say, "Thanks for coming over. For making the walk." I'm smiling, even though I know she can't see it.

I think she might be smiling back, but I can't tell for sure. "Yeah," she says. "It's good to see you."

"You too," I say. "I feel like you're a celebrity or something. Like, I've seen you on my laptop screen and phone screen so many times. It's so bizarre to like actually see you in person!"

I can't tell when she's smiling at me, but I can tell when she furrows her eyebrows at me, which is what she's doing now. She gives a little laugh. "That's . . . interesting."

I immediately regret saying it.

We just look at each other some more. "Hey, thanks again for the mask!" I eventually say.

"Oh yeah, no problem. I made a bunch. Some for my cousins. And Lucy's Girl Scout troop, of course."

"Cool," I say. Then, "Oh, gosh, will there be any kind of funeral for your great-aunt?"

"My great-aunt?" Again, the furrowed eyebrows.

"You mentioned cousins, so it made me think of your great-aunt."

"Oh, it's cousins on my dad's side that I made masks for."

That doesn't really answer my question, but I'm afraid of saying anything else that is wrong, so I just don't say anything at all.

"Do you want to walk some more?" she asks.

"Yeah, good idea."

She takes off again, and I manage to keep up with her this time. She keeps walking, and then we see two people walking toward us on the sidewalk. Vanessa turns to me and says something, but of course I can't hear her through the mask. She looks both ways, crosses the street, and I check the street, then cross behind her like an obedient puppy.

But when we cross, more people are walking toward us, so we cross again.

"It's like that game Frogger," I say.

"What?" she asks.

"It's like that game—"

"No, I heard you. I just don't know the game you're talking about."

I don't actually either; my dad has just made jokes about it before. All I know is, it's an old video game.

We're back to the boarded-up bodega again. She looks at me expectantly.

"It doesn't matter," I say.

She takes her phone out, I think to check the time, but then I see her fingers moving. She's texting someone.

I wait until she's done. "I should probably head back soon anyway. My parents didn't really want me to be gone more than an hour," she says.

"Yeah, same."

We just look at each other. The six feet between us feels like sixty.

"I'll walk you part of the way back?" she finally says.

"Sure, yeah, thanks."

She takes off, and I follow behind her again. When we're a few blocks from my apartment, she turns toward me. "I'm going to head back to my place."

"Okay." I take a step toward her. It's so automatic to want to hug her good-bye, kiss her good-bye, touch her in any kind of way.

She quickly backs away from me, putting her hands up.

"Right, sorry," I say.

"It's okay. Sorry for backing up. It's not personal."

But somehow, it does feel personal.

"I know." I feel foolish for making such an easy mistake. It's wild to me that this is a person who I used to kiss, hug. Now I can't even get close to her, see the bottom part of her face.

"See you later?" she says, waving.

"Yep, see you later." I watch her walk away, and all I want to do is cry. And I'm not even sure why.

I walk slowly home.

A few minutes later, I get a text.

Vanessa:

That was weird.

Claire:

Very.

Vanessa:

I don't think I realized how weird social distancing would be with you.

I want to tell her that I worry it wasn't just the social distancing, that it was us too.

Claire:

Yeah, for sure.

The blue dots stop and start a few times, but then nothing. I don't have anything else to say either.

When I get back to my street, it seems so empty, so quiet. Sadie isn't on her fire escape. I head up my stoop, up my stairs. I'm so hot, and my face still feels all wet, and even though I've hardly left my apartment in over a month, that's suddenly the only place I want to be.

I walk upstairs to the third floor, too quickly. I start to wipe the sweat off my forehead, then remember that I shouldn't touch my face. I open the door, and my parents are standing in the hallway, right by the front door.

My mom opens her mouth, but I quickly say, "I know, I'm washing my hands right now."

She looks hurt. "I wasn't going to say that. I was going to ask how Vanessa is, how it was to see her."

My dad says, "But maybe you could wash your hands while you tell us."

I roll my eyes at him but walk down the hall to the kitchen sink. I turn on the faucet and scrub my hands and arms for forty seconds. My parents stand right behind me as I say, "It was fine."

Which isn't a total lie. It was just that, fine. Not bad, not good, just fine.

I finish scrubbing, then dry my hands, and finally, finally rip off my mask. I breathe in the air, wipe off my sweaty face, and suddenly, it hits me again. "How do health care workers breathe in these things all day?"

"I don't know. But I'm glad they do," my mom says, with that crying look on her face. My dad looks at me pointedly.

"Vanessa is doing well!" I quickly say. "And it was good to see her. It was hard that we couldn't touch or get too close to each other, but it was still so nice to see each other in person rather than over a screen."

I look at my mom, but it's too late. She's wiping her eyes. "I'm so glad to hear that, honey," she says quietly.

"Mom, it's okay," I say impatiently. Why do I always feel like I'm managing everyone's emotions, everyone's expectations, except my own? "I'm going to take a shower."

"Okay, good idea," my mom says. I look at her, trying to figure out if she's going to cry more, but she says, "I'm fine! Just go get in the shower!"

"Okay," I say uncertainly.

I take a really long, really hot shower. For every part of my body that I scrub, I picture a whole bunch of germs dying, drowning.

I blow-dry my hair, too, picturing more germs dying in a heat wave.

I go back to my room. I pick up my phone, expecting some texts, but there's nothing. Not even from Vanessa. I tell myself it's because we just saw each other. But that had never stopped her before.

I also don't have any texts from Sadie either. Why would I? I just saw her too.

I open my laptop, click around on social media, but quickly close it again. I look across the street; the fire escape is empty. I think again about what it was like to see Sadie, to be even a few feet closer to her.

I pick up a sketchbook, start drawing. I draw Sadie exactly like I saw her earlier today. Her above me, being closer to her, seeing her from a different point of view, in person. Not from across the street, or over a laptop or phone screen.

Then I think about the blank look she gave me, and I stop drawing. I'm suddenly exhausted, so I go to bed without saying good night to anyone or checking anything on Babble.

When I wake up the next morning, I don't have any texts. Which is kind of weird. Vanessa didn't text to say good night to me. Then again, I didn't say good night to her either. Maybe she was exhausted, like me?

Also no texts from Sadie. Not that she needs to say good night to me or anything, but I thought she might want to say *something* after seeing me up close? Then again, I was with my girlfriend. My girlfriend, who I haven't told her about. My girlfriend, who also doesn't know about Sadie.

I scrunch my eyes closed. I wish I could just go back to sleep.

My phone buzzes with a text.

Vanessa:

Good morning.

Claire:

Good morning.

And then . . . nothing.

Claire:

I was really tired last night.

Vanessa:

Yeah, me too. We're making chicken pot pie for dinner tonight, and are going to make the crust at lunch, so I can't talk on our lunch break today.

She doesn't mention our date at all, but really, what is there to say? Maybe she just needs some space after yesterday? Even though it feels like all we've had lately is space.

Claire:

Okay.

Vanessa:

I look at my phone, waiting for more, but that's it.

Still no texts from Sadie either.

I check my email, but I can't process the number of people who have commented on my latest post, so I choose not to. I get dressed, get ready for school, and try not to look at the fire escape across the street.

It's surprisingly hard to do.

Especially because I don't see Sadie at all. On the fire escape, or in any texts on my phone.

After school, I try to work on homework, but my willpower breaks and I finally open up Babble to read the latest batch of comments from my post last night.

Ummm, where was Clarissa going??

Do you think she was going to see Sadie?

OMG, if she did, she better update already!

Sounds like Sadie is lonely. I bet Clarissa could keep her company.

Not digging these vague posts lately.

She gets vaguer and vaguer.

I'm losing interest.

I still think she's a fake.

I really don't care.

UPDATE PLEASE!

I scroll down, and there are thousands of comments.

While I'm scrolling, my phone chimes, and I'm so relieved it's a text, not another email letting me know about another comment on my Babble post.

Vanessa:

Want to work on homework together?

Claire:

Okay.

I'm actually surprised Vanessa stills want to do homework together after our weird date. It both bugs me and reassures me.

She video-calls me, and I answer the call, not totally sure what to expect, not totally sure what kind of mood she'll be in.

"Hey," I say carefully.

"Hey, babe," she says. She smiles, and it's nice to see her smile, to see the bottom half of her face. I just wish it didn't have to be over a video screen.

"Everything is okay with us, right?" I blurt out.

"Yes, of course; why wouldn't it be?" She looks surprised.

"Just wanted to make sure."

I should say, "Because yesterday was our weirdest date ever. And not just because we couldn't touch each other and were wearing masks. The distance between us felt much bigger than six feet." I should tell her about Sadie, that I'm the one writing the Babble posts. About everything. But I don't. I just say, "I was just making sure." I try to smile.

Vanessa smiles back, but it's another one of those smiles that is usually saved for someone she doesn't know very well. Then she opens her American history book and looks up at me. "You going to start your homework?"

"Right." I open my American history book too.

I'm trying really hard to read about the Cold War, but my mind keeps wandering. Out of habit, I look out my window across the street. Sadie still isn't on her fire escape. But wait, I can finally see her! She's sitting on her bed. I can see her glowing phone in her hand. I wonder what she's doing, if she's texting someone, playing a game, looking at pictures. I wonder why I haven't heard from her all day. I look back at my screen, and Vanessa is watching me.

"Did you say something?" I ask.

"Yeah, I asked how your homework was going," she says.

"Oh, sorry. I guess my mind was somewhere else."

"Okaaay," she says. "Where do you think that somewhere else was?"

"I guess I was just thinking about yesterday. About seeing you. Seeing you made me think about all of this again," I admit. "Missing you. About school being closed for the rest of the year."

"Yeah," she says, reading something on her screen. Then she smiles.

"What are you smiling at?"

"It's just a text." Vanessa looks startled. "You're on it too."

I really don't care what any of our friends have to say, unless it's something along the lines of lockdown is ending and school is starting again and life can go back to normal again.

"It's so nuts we might not be able to go to school this fall," I say. "Like, it's only spring now. That's so far away, the fall. Our senior year. And it's the whole country. It's so many schools. I hate this."

Vanessa is typing, smiling, and doesn't hear me at first.

"How can you be so calm about all this?" I ask.

"Babe, there is no point in freaking out. That's not going to help things any."

"I know that!" I snap.

"Why are you so worked up about this? We can still see each other on video chats. Go for walks like we did yesterday. Watch movies, do homework together. In the meantime, you can keep working on college stuff. Did you get a chance to look at the financial aid for Dartmouth and Amherst College?"

I don't want to go for walks around the neighborhood where I run after her, where we can't hear each other's voices through our masks. Where we can't touch each other, even get close to each other. I don't want to watch movies together through our phone and laptop screens. I don't want to constantly feel like I'm losing in whatever competition it is we're having, with the baking and cooking and family yoga. I don't want to think about college, about financial aid, because I don't even know if college is an option anymore since I don't know if my family can afford it. But I don't know how to tell Vanessa any of this.

I watch her smiling to herself, typing away, and wonder if she'd even hear me if I told her how I felt. I decide probably not.

"I think I need to go," I say suddenly.

Vanessa looks surprised. "Did you finish your homework already?"

"No, I didn't."

"So why are you going, then?" she asks, wrinkling her eyebrows at me. "Are you feeling okay? Are you still having trouble sleeping? I thought you looked a little tired yesterday on our walk."

"You saw like a quarter of my face!" I can't help but say.

She narrows her eyes at me. "Well, I saw the tired part. Your eyes."

"Fine, yeah, I'm tired," I say impatiently.

Vanessa is looking at something on her screen again that isn't me.

"I'm going to go."

Vanessa is still smiling to herself as she types.

"Bye?" I say uncertainly.

"Oh, bye, babe," she says, looking back over at me. She's completely distracted as she leans over to disconnect the call.

I open the email app on my phone, and there are still more comments on my Babble page. But I don't care. I don't want to read them. I'm tired of caring. I'm tired of responding to people's requests, giving in to their demands.

I shake my head, trying to clear it, and I look across the street.

31

Posted by Clarissareads:

Sadie is on her fire escape, book in hand. She told me recently that she's rereading all of Margaret Atwood's books. It looks like she just started a new one. I tap on my window, and she looks up, smiles at me, waves.

I smile and wave back, then climb out onto my fire escape.

My phone vibrates with a video call. Sadie.

"Are you okay?" she asks.

It kind of hurts my brain to see her on the fire escape across the street *and* on my phone screen. Hurts in a good way.

"Why wouldn't I be okay?" I say. More irritably than I mean to. "Sorry."

"Well, for one, you're a little snippy. And two, I don't know, something looked off about you from across the street, and seeing you close up on the screen, something looks even more off."

I sigh. "Has anyone ever told you that you're incredibly observant?"

She stands up on the fire escape and gives a little curtsy. "Perhaps once or twice. So what's up?"

"Fine. I don't want to lie. I'm terrible. Like, terrible, terrible. Not regular terrible."

I see the faintest hint of a smile dance across Sadie's face before she says, "Why? Only if you want to tell me."

"I do want to tell you," I say honestly, looking into those green eyes on my screen, then up across the street. "I just wish there were more to tell. I'm feeling kind of hopeless about everything. More so than usual? I miss getting brunch on the weekends from the diner; I miss the subway. I really miss not worrying all the time. Like, how did I ever take any of that for granted?"

Sadie nods as I talk. "Hugging people. Smelling food cooking in restaurants. Seeing kids playing together at a crowded playground." She's quiet for a second and then blurts out, "Hey, if lockdown were suddenly over, like really over, what would be the first thing you would do?"

"Do we still have to wear masks?" I ask.

"No, no masks, no social distancing, none of that."

"So is there a vaccine? How effective is it?"

She wrinkles her nose at me. "Okay, I'll try again. Sayyyy, the virus is just over. Like, everyone is cured."

"Well, how long has it been? How old am I?"

"Did anyone ever tell you that you ask too many questions?"

"Actually, no," I say, laughing.

"Hmm, I believe that," she says, laughing too.

"What's the first thing you'd do?" I ask her.

She shakes her head. "No way, I want to hear your answer first."

"Well, then you're going to have to wait and watch me think, because I'm really not sure."

"Fine with me," she says. She makes a big show of putting her head on her hand and gazing into the camera at me. It's actually super intense and over-whelming, but then she smiles, which makes me smile, and then starts laughing, which makes me start laughing. Which makes her laugh harder, which makes me laugh harder.

Every time one of us looks up at the camera or at each other across the street, we start laughing all over again. Finally, I take some deep breaths, and I manage to say, "Okay, I'm ready to answer your question."

"Well, took you long enough," Sadie says, starting to laugh again.

"I'd go to my favorite art supply store to get some new pencils and another sketchbook. Then I'd go to go my favorite bookstore, see what's new, agonize over which new book to get, finally decide on one. Maybe two. Then I'd get frozen hot chocolate and start read-ing one of my new books. And oh, I'd take the subway to all these places. And I wouldn't worry if someone was closer than six feet to me. And if the subway was running slow, or if the bookstore was crowded or if the café was out of my frozen hot chocolate? I wouldn't be mad."

She's quiet for a second. "Wow. All of that sounds... amazing."

"Well, it's the truth. It's the things I miss doing the most." I clear my throat. "Soooo, what about you? What would be your ideal day, if this was all over or whatever?"

"Hmm, well, I'd give my mom a hug. That's for sure. And hug my friends. And I guess I need to think where my ideal day would be. I mean, if it were back home in Massachusetts, I'd want to go to the movies with friends. After I hugged them all. And then we'd go to our favorite diner. And then I'd go home and tell my mom all about it. Face-to-face, not over a screen."

"I'm sorry," I say.

"You know, you say you're sorry a lot. For things that are totally not your fault."

I automatically say, "I'm sorry."

Sadie gives me a look, and I quickly say, "I'm sorry for saying 'I'm sorry'!"

She smiles. "That's better. Anyway, my ideal day in Brooklyn. I don't really know a lot about this neighborhood. Like, I know all the New York City things. My mom and I visit every year, and I know this place in Chinatown I like. But my ideal day here? It'd be exploring this neighborhood. Walking around. Without a mask. And oh, there's that pizza place around the corner. I'd like a slice from there too."

"Mario's!" I say, smacking my head. "How could I forget about pizza from there?"

She laughs. "So maybe our ideal days could overlap. We could meet for pizza."

I smile. I can't help it. "I'd like that," I say.

Sadie quietly says, "Me too."

And then neither of us says anything for a while.

Likes: 41,980

Comments: 13,167

32

Somehow, even after the weird date with Vanessa, the weirdness of the last few days, I actually sleep well. I mean, I still wake up a lot, but I do manage to fall asleep again. Probably because I don't check my phone at all. Probably because I put my phone in airplane mode and turn my laptop off.

When my alarm goes off for school, my room is still dark. I closed my light-blocking curtains really tight, I guess.

I drag myself out of bed, take a deep breath, and turn airplane mode on my phone back off. I open my curtain, and I'm surprised to see that it's rained. I wonder, are masks waterproof?

I don't feel like thinking about it anymore, though, so I open up my email app on my phone, scroll through comments.

I love Clarissa's ideal day!

Obvs she's saying it's something she wants to do with Sadie.

OMGGG I wish one of them would ask the other one out already! What are they waiting for?

Almost enough to make up for that obv fake picture of Clarissa.

Well, not like anyone can go anywhere soon, anyway. No rush?

So wait, we still don't know where Clarissa was going? I was hoping it was out to see Sadie, but didn't seem like it?

So, aha, we know they're in Brooklyn.

We kinda already knew that anyway?

This proves they live in Brooklyn!

No it doesn't! Any of that stuff can be easily googled.

I mean Brooklyn pizza is the best.

No way, deep dish is better.

I love their chats, but I feel like they need a DATE already.

And wait, hold up, we still don't know why Clarissa was fighting with her parents!!

And yeah, where was she going??

So they are pretty much asking each other on a date when the virus is over?

Yeah but who knows when that'll be.

I dunno if I want to read about their video chats for the next year. No offense.

Hellllllo, anyone ever heard of social distancing?

If they have masks they could see each other, duh.

Well, one of them needs to step up their game.

And as usual lately, the comments don't make me feel any better about anything. I want to tell these Internet strangers that they're being way too nosy, way too demanding, that I don't owe them anything. That they should all get a hobby that doesn't involve me. That Sadie is just a friend. That I wasn't talking about a date when I talked about my ideal day. Obviously. That my girlfriend and I are fighting, and I miss her, and I miss my old life. I miss everyone's old life. And I really want to write about how I saw Sadie up close in person, but I don't, because then I'll have to talk about my girlfriend, and I'll have to explain why I haven't mentioned her before, and I don't know why I haven't. And I'll have to talk about the blank stare Sadie gave me. And how I didn't hear from her that night after she saw me with my girlfriend. But I'm tired. Too tired. And I just don't feel like thinking about any of it anymore.

Instead, I take out my sketchbook.

I think again about seeing Sadie from a different angle. Looking up at her. Not from a laptop or phone screen.

I open my sketchbook, start drawing.

I draw myself standing in front of my building. I draw my stoop, with the cracked step, my wrought-iron fence. I draw Sadie above me. Sadie has a halo, looking down at me. I draw the fire escape, but part of it is made of clouds. I draw her building, and I put little rays of light shooting out of the stoop, out of the front door.

When my stomach starts growling, I finally put my sketchbook down on my desk and head out to the kitchen for some breakfast.

But it's like our kitchen shelves have exploded. There are cans of food, bags of baking things, and jars of spices everywhere.

My mom is sitting on the floor, and she's looking at a label maker in her hand, muttering to herself. When did we get a label maker?

"Um, Mom?"

She looks up. "Ah! Claire! Can you help me with this darn thing? I think it's jammed."

"Are you okay?" I ask, looking at her closely.

"Me? Oh, I'm fine! I was just going to try to finish rearranging all this stuff in this cabinet. What do you think about shelf paper?"

"I think I have no idea what shelf paper is."

She laughs. "It's decorative. Paper to put on your shelves to make them look pretty."

"Why do you want shelves to look pretty, though? They're shelves. And won't they be covered anyway, since they're, you know, shelves?"

Just then my dad emerges from the bedroom, his black-and-gray hair sticking up. He looks slightly shell-shocked. He turns to me, eyes wide. "Your mom is after me to go through the clothes on my side of the closet, and it's a lot." He runs his hands through his hair, making it stick up even more.

"I am not after you," my mom says, whirling around to look at my dad. "I'm reminding you of your responsibilities as a living, breathing adult in this apartment!" But then she smiles, and my dad smiles back, and I wonder what Sadie would think if she met them, watched them interact. But then I wonder why I'm thinking about Sadie at all, why I'm thinking about Sadie meeting my parents.

My dad goes back to their bedroom, and my mom starts taking more stuff out of the cabinet. "Um, Mom, do you want help?" I ask half-heartedly. "I could help you at lunch." Usually Vanessa and I video-chat over our lunch breaks, but I don't know if she even wants to talk to me after our tense conversation yesterday. She hasn't texted me since. And maybe reorganizing the kitchen might be a nice change. I'm sure she'd understand. If anything, she'd probably encourage it, seeing as how much time she likes to spend with her family, cooking, baking, doing yoga. Organizing isn't making a crepe cake, but it's a start.

"No, don't worry about it. This is going to be super boring," she says, her back to me as she pulls out a can of tomato soup and examines it.

I think about all the cooking and meal planning she's been doing since the pandemic started, all her worrying about job stuff, and how she let me go on the date with Vanessa, and I say, "No, Mom, I'll help over my lunch break. It'll be . . . fun!" I try to put some enthusiasm into my voice.

She turns back around, looks at me skeptically. "Okay, but only if you're sure."

"Totally." I hope that my smile is convincing enough. Then I make a smoothie from another one of her packs and go back to my room.

As I log in to my remote classroom, just before I put my phone in airplane mode, I send Vanessa a quick text.

Claire:

Helping my mom with something at lunch. Talk to you after classes?

I keep my phone in airplane mode while my teachers are talking, but I still keep pulling it out of my pocket, flipping it over in my hands. I wonder if Vanessa has sent me a message yet.

The morning drags by. Everyone is restless, and my teachers keep having to repeat themselves.

Finally, it's English class, and then finally, finally, I have forty minutes of freedom.

I flip my phone back on, and there's a text from Vanessa. I expect a full summary of her day so far, or maybe even an *I'm sorry for downplaying your anxiety,* but there's just *OK.*

OK. Two letters, just like *hi.*

I think I like *hi* better.

I start a text to her: *Sorry for freaking out yesterday!* But why should I apologize for getting upset about something related to the pandemic?

I'm tired of apologizing for things I don't need to be sorry for.

I put my phone down and head out to the kitchen. My mom has huge mounds of kitchen towels and oven mitts in front of her. She picks up a towel from one pile, examines it, and puts it in another pile.

"Mom?"

She turns to look at me, another towel in her hand. "Oh, hey, Claire. You ready for lunch?"

"No, Mom, not yet. Remember I actually wanted to help you?"

She laughs. "I thought you might change your mind. But really, why?"

I shrug. Because I can't sit in front of my laptop anymore. Because I can't read any more comments on my Babble posts. Because I can't send or read any more texts. Because I don't feel like thinking about whatever it is that's going on with Vanessa and me. Because I don't feel like thinking about college or money. But I say, "You've done a lot for Dad and me. And you let me go on that date with Vanessa. And you look like you need some help."

My mom sighs, says, "Yeah, perhaps I do. But like I said, this is super boring. You should enjoy your youth!"

"Mom, remember that whole pandemic thing? I can't exactly enjoy my youth at the moment."

My mom stops laughing, and she says, "I'm so sorry, Claire," with this really serious look on her face.

"Mom, it's okay," I say, a little impatiently. "Just let me help you, okay?"

"Okay," she agrees.

"So, what is it exactly that you're doing?" I ask, looking at the piles of fabric in front of her.

"Aha. I am, my dear, organizing. Spring cleaning. Decluttering. Finding out what sparks joy."

"Oh," I say, waiting for further instruction.

My dad walks out of their room, wearing a tank top that I've never seen before. A tight rainbow-striped tank top. "Is that Mom's?" I ask.

"What? No, it's mine! I wore it to my very first Pride parade when I was nineteen," he says proudly. He tugs on it. "It shrunk in the wash a little, but it's definitely still wearable." He lifts his arms, and I see his belly hair poking out.

"Ew, Dad, put your arms down," I say.

"Yeah, Joe, we're busy," my mom says, rolling her eyes.

"Melissa, did you rope your poor, precious, innocent daughter into this mess?" my dad asks.

"No! She roped herself. I mean, volunteered herself," my mom says, shooting me a quick smile.

"Whew! Better you than me!" my dad says, backing up toward their bedroom. "See you later!"

My mom laughs a little, then hands me part of one of the piles in front of her. "Here you go," she says.

"Um, what do you want me to do with this?"

"Oh, right! Just look through it. We have way too many linens that are falling apart. Find any that seem like they have too many holes.

Then put them over here in the rag pile," she says, pointing to another stack. "And the ones that are still okay can be folded up, put over here," she says, pointing to another stack.

"That's it?" I ask.

"That's it."

I get to work examining, folding, stacking, organizing. It's not exactly my idea of fun, but it is nice to give my brain something else to think about besides Babble, besides Vanessa, besides Sadie.

"Thanks for helping me with this," my mom says. "Your dad is working on his part of the closet today. I'm hoping to finish up the kitchen by the weekend, and then tackle the bathroom over the weekend." She says it with a little bit of a gleam in her eye.

"Why are you doing all this?" I ask.

She looks surprised. "What do you mean? It needed to be done."

"Really?" I ask skeptically.

"Well, maybe not needed. Like, the apartment isn't going to fall over if I don't organize its contents. But yeah, we could use some tidying up. Also, it's kind of a good distraction?"

"Distraction?" I repeat.

"Yeah, from worrying about the virus, from reading the news, from thinking about what's happening all over the world, from thinking about my work, from thinking about which freelance client to email next. It's good to focus my brain power somewhere else." She sighs. "And sometimes you just have to make a big mess of something in order to get it cleaned up again."

"Mom, that makes no sense," I say, laughing.

She waves her hand. "No, I mean it! Sometimes you just need to empty out all your cabinets, all your insides, examine what you find, and then put it back inside again. When you're done, you have a clean, organized cabinet. But it's a messy, long process. But a messy, long, necessary process."

"Are we still talking about cabinets?"

My mom smiles and winks at me. "Of course."

I watch her folding, thinking how this would be the perfect time to tell her about my Babble posts, about Sadie, tell her about how I wanted to keep myself distracted with the posts and that things got out of hand, but I can't bring myself to say the words. Because talking about it will mean thinking about it, and I just don't want to. I just want to think about towels for a little bit.

"Also," my mom says, "it's nice to feel like I have control over something."

"What do you mean, control?"

"I mean, I can't control anything about this darn virus, or anything happening outside the walls of this apartment right now; I can't control that I was furloughed. So since I can't control what happens outside it, I might as well control what happens inside it. Does that even make sense?"

It makes too much sense.

My mom is looking at me, and I quickly say, "Yeah, it does."

"Good," she says. "We're all just trying to muddle through the best we can, right?"

"Right," I say weakly.

"I understand the baking thing everyone is doing now too," my mom goes on. She's examining a bag of flour. "Who knew that flour expired? Huh. Maybe I'll make a trip to the store this afternoon? I don't feel like waiting for a grocery delivery."

I'm not really listening, though. My mind is back on Sadie, back on Babble again. Maybe my mind never left. I look at my piles of organized and folded dish towels and oven mitts. "Um, I just need to go check something on my computer."

My mom laughs. "Honey, you don't need to make up excuses if you don't want to do this anymore."

"No, it's not that—"

"Claire, I'm your mom. I know you better than you realize. Go chill out in your room. Isn't your lunch break almost over, anyway? There's a tuna sandwich in the fridge for you."

"Okay. And thanks, Mom." I stand up. "For letting me go on the date with Vanessa."

"You're welcome. I can't even imagine how much you must have missed her."

"Yeah." And I did. I still do. But I'm realizing the Vanessa I miss is the Vanessa from before lockdown. I miss the Vanessa I could touch, hug, sit next to. The Vanessa I could have shared experiences with that existed outside a computer or a phone screen. This Vanessa that I'm constantly video-chatting with, that I constantly feel like I'm in some kind of losing competition with, that I'm now also constantly arguing with . . . sometimes she doesn't feel like the same person I started the relationship with six months ago.

My mom is looking at me closely. "My offer still stands. You can talk to me or your dad about anything. You know that, right?"

"Yeah, Mom," I say. "No offense, though. Dad gives awful advice."

She groans. "I can't believe he told you not to talk to Vanessa for up to a week."

"Where did he get that from?" I ask. "Like, what century?"

My mom laughs. "You know he means well, right?"

My dad emerges from their bedroom again, this time in jeans and a

T-shirt that he is trying to tug down over his belly. "Look! Had this shirt for twenty years, and it still fits me! Good thing, too, since I now look twenty years younger after my face mask."

My mom and I look at him and start laughing.

"What's so funny?" he asks, looking genuinely confused.

"Nothing, Joe," my mom says. But then she cracks up all over again, and I laugh even harder.

I go back to my room, still laughing, while my dad tugs on his shirt, still looking confused, still not looking twenty years younger.

After my slow afternoon classes, I turn my phone back on. I ignore the rapidly increasing number on my email app, but I can't ignore that I don't have any new texts.

Claire:

Hi.

I text tentatively. That word was so powerful in my texts with Sadie.

Vanessa:

And then nothing.

Claire:

Homework?

It seems like the right thing to text.

Vanessa:

> Would love to, babe, but Lucy and I are making more masks for her Girl Scout troop, and for her friend's Girl Scout troop. Will probably need to skip our bedtime chat too.

So she's not mad at me? I feel relieved, and then I smile. It's really sweet they're making masks. My girlfriend is really sweet. I have a really awesome girlfriend. Who cares if she's not a wreck about this virus? Who cares if she's so good at lockdown? Maybe I've been overreacting.

Claire:

> No problem, babe.

Vanessa:

I put my phone down, take a look around my room. I think my mom is onto something with this whole organizing and tidying and cleaning thing. I poke around my dresser for a little bit, start refolding some shirts, and my mom is right, it *is* a good distraction. It *is* nice to have control over something.

Suddenly, things seem almost okay.

I hum to myself as I sort a pile of skirts.

I'm in such a good mood that I decide I should just take a quick peek at the latest comments on my Babble posts. I haven't checked since this morning.

But as I read, my good mood instantly dissipates.

I think she's a big fake. About everything.

She needs to prove she's real. A better picture. A picture of Sadie. A video.

Something. Anything.

Something where we can see her face.

Yeah. We need a picture of Sadie.

I agree. Clarissa is being creepy. She needs to tell Sadie she's writing about her!

Yeah! Clarissa needs to tell Sadie before someone else does.

Over it.

Chill out, guys. Don't forget this is an actual person we're talking about.

Is it?

If she goes on a date with Sadie, maybe I'll believe her.

So? Anyone can say they went on a date with someone.

If she can somehow prove that she goes on a date with Sadie, I'll believe her.

How is she going to do that?

She's smart. I'm sure she'll think of something.

Is she smart, though? I think her writing is only kinda okay.

Yeah, the writing stinks.

I still think they're not real people.

I don't even know if I care if it's real or not anymore?

BORING.

I close my laptop, feeling completely creeped out and completely annoyed. And, I hate to admit it, completely hurt. First they liked my posts. Then they wanted a picture. Then they weren't happy with the picture. Then they called me a fake and doubted my existence and Sadie's existence, and now they're telling me my writing isn't good. It's boring.

These posts were supposed to be fun for me to write. Used to be something fun for me to write. It was supposed to be a distraction, something else for me to think about besides a rapidly spreading deadly virus that has no cure. It was supposed to be something to make me happy. And now it's just turned into a big mess that makes me feel terrible. I wish I hadn't ever started the Sadie posts.

If I write another post, whatever I write won't be enough for people, and I'm just going to get more comments from more people asking for more pictures, more proof that I am who I say am. Probably more people saying I'm a bad writer.

Maybe I should just delete all the posts? But that will just make people think I'm a fake even more. It'll just prove their theories.

I open up my laptop again, and I go to the "settings" part on my Babble account's home page. I scroll until I find the delete account button. I hover my cursor over the button. But I just can't do it. I've had this Babble account since I was thirteen, and it only contained mediocrely written book reviews before the Sadie posts, but still, it's *my* Babble account. My little piece of myself on the Internet.

As I think, my phone lights up with a text.

Vanessa:

> Just so you know, everyone thinks you're overreacting too. About there maybe not being any school. About everything. Mira and I are going to hang out next week too.

And just like that, whatever little bit of happiness, peace, I felt is completely, totally gone.

Which makes what happens next even harder.

33

Posted by Clarissareads:

I can barely process what just happened. Like, my hands are shaking right now. Okay, deep breaths. So, my mom and I went to the grocery store tonight. It's yet another one of those things we all used to do all the time and not think twice about. We'd touch things, get close to people, go into a crowded store, we'd grab just a roll of paper towels if we needed them, we'd go shopping at 9:00 p.m. We'd go into a store, no matter how full, no fifty-percent capacity, no waiting on lines to get in the store. It was just one of those things we never gave much thought to before the pandemic. One of the many things we never gave much thought to. It's all so complicated now.

Anyway, I'm in my room after dinner when my mom asks me if I want to go to the grocery store with her.

"Sure, I'll go with."

My mom looks a little relieved. "Great. I'm buying flour and sugar and eggs. They're heavy! And breakable! And maybe it'll be good for us both to get out of the house?"

I haven't left the apartment much, except for short

morning walks with her. So strange I'm now used to being home all the time.

"Yeah, probably a good idea," I say.

"Great! Want to go now? If not, no rush, of course!" She laughs. It's funny and not funny. So not funny it is funny. So funny it's not funny anymore.

My mom and I put on our masks, throw some sanitizer in our bags, and we are out the door. Outside! I look up at the fire escape right away. It's really weird to see it up close, in person. It's like being at a play and then getting close to the stage when it's over. But this stage is empty. No actors. No Sadie.

It's a warm, almost humid, spring night, almost 7:00, and usually the sidewalks would be packed with people on their way to dinner, the movies, the city. And now there is just...no one. With the empty streets, the empty sidewalks, my mom and I not talking much, everything is just...quiet. I realize I hear birds chirping. It's creepy and weird, and I'm starting to regret agreeing to go with my mom.

When we turn the corner to get to the store, we see the line. I feel my mom stiffen next to me.

But we get on line, and it's ten people deep. Which I don't know if it is a lot or a little because I've never waited on line to get into a grocery store in a pandemic before.

It moves quickly, though, and we're inside the store. And it's so weird. There are arrows on the floor all over the place, telling people which way to go, and the cashiers have sheets of plastic around their work-stations. I'm taking it all in, and I guess my mom is, too, because she's not really looking where she's going, and a man tells her she's too close to him. She starts to say she's sorry, but he walks away before she finishes her apology.

I can tell my mom is annoyed, and my mom can tell I can tell she's annoyed, but we just act like it didn't happen.

And that's when something does happen. About fifteen feet away from me, I see a teenage girl with dark hair, with half of it shaved, and it's Sadie. Sadie!

My mom is looking at oranges, and Sadie is putting some apples in a produce bag, her back to me.

I start to walk over to her, then stop when I realize I'm getting too close. I say, "Sadie!" But I guess I don't say it loud enough; I mean, the mask makes it hard to hear, because she doesn't turn around.

I can't exactly tap her on the shoulder, and then while I'm standing there, thinking what I should do, she spins around quickly, and she's facing me. She looks right at me, and I can't believe I'm seeing Sadie in person, up close! I've seen her face over a screen, and I've seen her from across the street, on her fire escape, but this is her, in the flesh, in person. Close. It takes my breath away for a second.

But it's weird, because she just looks at me like she

doesn't recognize me or something. It's so strange. But then I realize, I'm wearing the mask! She just keeps looking at me, and I keep looking at her, and then finally, she squints at me, and something like recognition crosses her face. It must have been the mask.

I get a little closer to her, still staying six feet apart.

"Not quite the slice of pizza at Mario's, is it?" I ask, grinning, even though she can't see my smile. I make sure to say it loud, because of the mask and all, but she still looks confused.

"You know, like the pizza we talked about? What we'd do if lockdown is over?"

I can't see her mouth, but I don't think she's smiling.

"So, what are you getting?" I ask awkwardly.

"Oh, I don't even know, actually. I just needed a quick change of scenery."

"Oh, cool."

She just keeps looking at me, and out of the corner of my eye I see my mom digging through a bin of oranges.

"I think my mom is going to bake. She needs orange juice. But wants to squeeze the oranges herself." I don't know why I'm telling her this, but I don't know what else to say or do.

She doesn't say anything, and then she looks behind me. I turn, and a masked customer is trying to squeeze by me in the narrow aisle, but there's no room, and the customer and I are doing this weird dance to not get close to each other.

When I turn around, Sadie is walking away toward the deli. Before I can really think about what I'm doing, I'm right behind her, or six feet behind her. She turns and looks surprised to see me again.

"I can't believe we're finally seeing each other in person!" I'm smiling, but I realize again she can't see my smile.

She nods, but then the woman behind the counter takes her order, and I just stand there, feeling weird.

It's like this Sadie is an entirely different person than the one I've been texting with, talking to over video chat. There's none of that ease, that comfort, I've gotten so used to. It's almost like I don't know her at all.

When she's done, she looks surprised again to see me. She says, "Don't you think you should find your mom?"

"Oh, yeah, um, I mean, I can still see her. She's getting apples now. But yeah, I guess I should go. It's good to see you. Really good to see you. And like, so bizarre, to actually see you closer than across the street!"

I immediately regret saying it. I feel dumb saying it. Wrong. Everything feels wrong and dumb.

She just looks at me.

"See you later," she says, saving me from my awkward self.

"Okay." I take a step toward her. After all this time of talking to her on the phone, over text, over video, she's like a magnet, and I can't help but be drawn to her.

She backs away from me, and I feel even stupider.

"Sorry!" I say.

"It's cool."

"I guess I'm just nervous to see you or something," I say, feeling my awkwardness seeping out of every pore.

She must not hear me again because she just waves, walking away, and gets on the checkout line.

My mom appears at my side, her handbasket full of produce. "Was that someone from school?"

"Um, no, not quite."

She looks at me, waiting for me to say more, but I quickly say, "Ready to get on line? We're not supposed to be in here too long, right?"

"Just need to grab a few more things."

So we finish up our shopping and get on line to pay, and then make the quiet walk back to the apartment.

And now I'm home. Still kinda shaking. Still kinda processing. I know it was just because of the mask that she didn't recognize me at first, and maybe she was in a bad mood or something, but I guess I thought things would have been different when I saw her. Oh well! Right?

I check my phone just now, thinking maybe I'll have a text from Sadie, but there's nothing from her.

Maybe there never was?

Likes: 35,803

Comments: 10,590

34

I have a dream that I'm on a date with Vanessa. We're walking around the neighborhood, and it's so good to see her, and we're talking and laughing. It's a beautiful sunny day, and the sidewalks are packed. Then I feel my face in my dream, realize I'm not wearing my mask, and Vanessa isn't wearing hers either. I look around at the crowds of people and realize none of them are in masks. A man a few feet in front of me stops on the sidewalk, turns around, and looking at me, starts coughing. Then the woman next to him turns to face me, too, and starts coughing. And then everyone on the crowded sidewalks is staring at me, coughing. Including Vanessa.

I wake up, sweating, breathing hard.

I have no idea what time is it, but I'm a little afraid if I fall asleep again I'm going to have the same dream, so I try to stay awake for a little bit, but eventually I doze off. I'm in and out of sleep, and then, finally, my alarm goes off for school. I turn the alarm on my phone off, then open my email app.

The emails poured in. Like, reallllly poured in. Apparently there are some comments on my Babble post. A lot of comments on my Babble post. I just . . . can't, though. Not yet. A text pops up, so I read that instead.

Vanessa:

> Good morning! OMG, I gotta send you this smoothie recipe that my mom made today. It had cocoa nibs and oatmeal in it!

Claire:

> Sounds yummy.

I don't like oatmeal, and I'm not entirely sure what a nib is. And I don't know why she's texting me about her breakfast, when the last thing she said to me was that I was overreacting about a pandemic, and that she was going to hang out with one of our friends.

Vanessa:

> It is. Talk after school? We're making another pot pie today at lunch. ☺

Claire:

> OK.

It just feels like the easiest thing to say.

I float through my breakfast, my morning classes, all while thinking about my email, the comments. I don't want to read what everyone has to say. I don't want proof that whatever I'm feeling for Sadie is tricky. I don't want confirmation that what happened at the grocery store with her didn't make any sense. I don't want to deal with how guilty

I feel. I have a girlfriend. A girlfriend who I can't seem to stop arguing with.

Finally, when my afternoon classes are done, I can't take it anymore. I breathe deeply and open my Babble page.

I've never had so many comments. So many comments. I take another deep breath, start reading. I can't figure out where to begin, so I start somewhere in the middle.

Ummm, what the heck was this all about?

What happened?

What is Sadie's problem?

So they don't like each other?

I guess she's just not that into you, Clarissa.

I'm so confused.

I've been on the edge of my seat for this?

I think Clarissa just got friend-zoned.

Wait, I thought they liked each other?

Maybe the fantasy was better than the reality?

So that was a total letdown.

What the heck did I just read?

How did they have no chemistry?

Okay, something is not lining up right.

Now what? Are they going to "break up"?

Going to be hard for them to avoid each other since they live across the street from each other.

Well, this could get awkward for them.

I'm so confused.

I don't understand.

I don't get it.

I don't really get it either.

I close my laptop, look across the street. There is no one on that fire escape.

My phone buzzes. This time not with an email or a new Babble comment, but a text.

Vanessa:

> I want to talk to you about something.

We always talk; why is she texting to tell me she wants to talk? I feel like my blood is turning into ice. I start to write back, but I'm shaking suddenly, and it takes a long time for my fingers to spell out, *What is it?*

A second later, my phone buzzes in my lap. I yelp. It's a video call from Vanessa.

My heart skips faster in my chest.

I answer, and she's got a really weird look on her face. Oh god.

"Hey," I say carefully. "Everything okay?"

"Hi!" she says brightly. Too brightly. "You will not believe the day I have had. There is so much going on. Like, I don't even know where to start. My mom always says to start at the beginning of the story, but I don't even know where the beginning of this story is! And I just have so many feelings about it all." She takes a deep breath. "Oh, just listen to me babble on and on. Babble, babble, babble."

The icy feeling spreads through my chest. "What did you say?"

"You heard me. I was apologizing for babbling. I do that a lot. Babble."

"Why do you keep saying that word?" I ask quietly.

"Which word?" she asks sweetly.

"Babble." I suddenly hate the word more than any other word I've heard or said in my life.

"Oh, I hadn't noticed," she says. "But thank you for pointing it out to me. Because that's one aspect of a successful relationship. An aspect that is really important to me. Honesty. Trust. Because girlfriends don't keep things from their girlfriends. And girlfriends certainly don't write Babble posts pretending to be someone else, pretending their girlfriend doesn't even exist. Girlfriends would never be that creepy. Whew, sorry, I really am babbling again, aren't I?"

There are so many things I want to say, need to say, but my brain isn't moving fast enough. "Who told you it was me?" I finally say. I don't know why it's what my brain decides my mouth should say.

I want to be mad at someone, blame someone. Even though deep down I know the only person to blame is myself.

She looks surprised. "Are you serious? No one had to tell me. I recognized your writing. Never knew your full name was Clarissa, but learn something new every day, right? I thought it might have been you for a while, especially when I saw how uncomfortable you were when I told you about the fire escape girl posts. I was waiting for you to tell me yourself. I was hoping you'd tell me on our date. But you didn't. I just read your last post about supposedly seeing Sadie in person . . . and I just can't keep it in anymore."

Now it's my turn to be surprised. "But you've never read anything I've written."

"Claire, I've been dating you for over six months. Talking to you every single day. I recognize your voice. You write just like you talk. And the way you think."

"But how do you know how I think?" I ask weakly.

"I think I know you better than you realize," she says quietly. "Is Sadie real?" she says even more quietly.

"You're too good for me!" I blurt out.

"Good for you?" she says, her voice full of disbelief. "What does that have to do with your posts? And that's like saying it's not you, it's me."

"Well, it kinda is?" I say.

"What kinda is?" she asks.

"It kinda is me, not you."

Tears fill her eyes. "Claire, what are you talking about? You're starting to scare me a little bit. What does any of this have to do with your Babble posts? And you still haven't answered my question: Is Sadie real?"

"No, listen, Vanessa. You *are* too good for me. You're smart, and nice, and organized, and you go to bed early and wake up early and you floss—"

"What do your Babble posts have to do with me flossing?"

"And you're just so . . . good. And I'm just not."

"You're not what? A good flosser? I'm so confused," she says, wiping away tears but also smiling a little.

"What? No, I floss sometimes, but it's not part of my daily routine.

But, ugh, I don't want to talk about flossing anymore! What I'm getting at is I'm not perfect, like you. You're full of neat, tidy corners, and I'm just a big old mess of rough edges."

"So you're a sculpture now?"

"Yes, I'm a sculpture who doesn't floss," I say. I realize how ridiculous it sounds, how ridiculous this conversation is, all of this is, and smile a little.

She smiles back. "So is this weird conversation over now? Can we go back to the part where you tell me why you hid your Babble account from me? Why you wrote about Sadie? And can you please just answer my question, Claire: Is Sadie real? She's not, right? This is all fiction?"

Her blue eyes peer into mine. I feel myself squirming. "Yes," I finally say. "She's real. I'm sorry," I say lamely.

Vanessa looks like I just slapped her. "Are you kidding me? That was her on the fire escape, the day we had our date. I didn't think it was, that she was real . . . Oh god, I'm such an idiot. I should have known." She says it barely above a whisper.

I take a deep breath. I think about how hard things have been with her. "I'm so sorry. I, just, sometimes I'm afraid to be myself with you. And I wasn't afraid to let Sadie in. To be myself." I say it really fast.

"And so what, you've been afraid to let me in? Claire, I am your girlfriend. You can tell me anything, be anything. That's how relationships are supposed to work. Well, good ones anyway."

"That's my point. You won't want to be in a relationship with me anymore if you find out what I'm really like."

She laughs as tears pour down her face. "Claire, what is it you think you're hiding? Or trying to hide? Unless you're telling me that you're really a spy, I think I know you better than you realize."

"Why don't you ever ask about my art? Or my writing? Or the books I'm reading?" I blurt out.

"What?" She looks genuinely shocked.

"You never ask about my art," I say. "You know I draw. I know you've seen my sketchbooks. You know I write, too, and that I read a lot. Why don't you ever ask me about any of that stuff?"

"Um, Claire, I hate to be the one to tell you this, but you know who is in charge of your wants and needs?" Her voice is shaking.

"What does that have to do with anything?"

"No, Claire. I want you to think about that. Answer the question. Who is in charge of determining your wants and needs?"

I don't know where she is going with this. "My parents, I guess."

"Okay, that's fair. I'll give you that one. You're not eighteen yet. You live with them. They're in charge of your safety, feeding you, all that stuff. But who is in charge of, hmm, deciding when you're hungry?" She suddenly sounds very calm, like she's talking to a toddler in the middle of a tantrum.

"My parents?" I ask hopefully.

"No. It's up to you to recognize when you're hungry. No one can really know if you're hungry except for you."

"Okay," I say, still confused about what she's getting at.

"So, if there is something you think you need or you think you want, whose responsibility is it to voice those needs and wants?"

"My parents?" I ask again, even though I have a pretty good feeling that's the wrong answer.

She looks at me but doesn't say anything.

"It's not my parents?" I finally ask.

"No, Claire," she says quietly. "It's you. If you're not happy with some aspect of our relationship, it's up to you to tell me."

"It's not that I wasn't happy!" I say.

"Right. You're totally happy. And I'm just supposed to mind-read that you want me to ask you about your art and your writing and what you're reading. Those both make total sense," she says, rolling her eyes.

"I guess I just thought you would have figured out that I wanted to show you my art, my writing. Talk about what I'm reading." As I say it, I realize how ridiculous it sounds. How ridiculous I'm being.

"Let me tell you something, Claire. Holding part of yourself back from the person you're dating? From friends? From anyone? It doesn't make you edgy, it doesn't make you different, it doesn't make you cool. It just makes you a big fake."

"I'm so sorry, Va—"

"No, no more apologies, Claire. It's way too late for that. I'm sorry if your fantasy life is better than real life, but this is me, here, not some made-up version of me. Not some fantasy-life version of me, or Sadie, or whoever, where you get to call the shots, where you get to be perfect. Good luck with Sadie." Then she ends the call.

I look at the phone in my hand, my head spinning. I think I feel sad. No, devastated. No, angry. But at who? Then I realize I'm feeling and thinking too much, and everything has just canceled itself out, and I feel mostly kind of numb.

My phone vibrates in my hand again, but it's like it's coming from somewhere really far away. Like, I'm somewhere near the ceiling of my room, looking down at myself holding the phone.

It's another video call. Sadie.

I shake my head, try to focus, and I answer the call.

"Hey," I say carefully.

"Hi," she says slowly.

And then we just look at each other.

"Okay, so if you're not going to tell me yourself, I guess I'll do it for you. I know about your posts. What the heck?" She doesn't even look mad, though. Just kind of confused?

"Who told you about them?" is the first question I think to ask.

"Who told me about them?" she asks. Her voice is so calm. "No one had to *tell* me about them. I am capable of reading things on the Internet myself."

"I thought you weren't on social media," I say dumbly.

"What?"

"When we first started talking, you said you weren't on social media much."

"Jeez, who knows what I said. I say a lot. Sometimes I forget what I've said five minutes ago. And no matter what I said, it's something I said. It's not like I signed a legal oath saying I was never going to go on social media."

"I know, but—"

"And even if I did say that, which I don't remember, it's my life, and you know who is in charge of my life?"

"You," I say quietly.

"That's right, me!" she says, still so calm. "I don't know what happened to you. Like, what makes you want to control people like that?"

"What? I wasn't trying to control you! That's the last thing I want to do."

"And you made it seem like we had some kind of relationship or something. I'm not like that. You have a girlfriend, don't you?"

"Wait, how did you know that? I didn't ever tell you about Vanessa."

"I'm not an idiot. I saw the picture of her that you have by your desk. I saw you guys go for a walk that day. I was waiting for you to bring her up. You never did."

"I'm sorry," I say again. I wonder how many times I've said those words today. My brain can't keep up, though. "So you knew I had a girlfriend?"

"And the way you wrote it, all these pauses between us, the quiet moments, all the gazing, I mean you wrote it to make it seem like it's something it's not," Sadie continues, like she didn't hear me. "You made me into someone I'm not. You made it seem like we have some kind of relationship that we don't." She's looking around, anywhere but at me as she talks. She looks almost bored.

"What are you talking about?" I ask, shaking again. But this time it's a full-body shiver. I should get a sweater, a hoodie, something, but I'm paralyzed.

"Look, you're cool, but what we had, well, it wasn't anything."

"It wasn't anything?" I say, fighting back tears.

She shrugs. "I mean, no?"

"But you opened up to me!"

"I open up to everyone," she says, shrugging again. "I thought I told you I don't believe in secrets."

"You mean, the way you talk to me is the way you talk to everyone?"

She looks confused. "Uh, yeah. Haven't I told you that I believe in honesty?"

"But—but . . . I don't open up to anyone the way I have to you. With you."

"Well, that's on you. Maybe you should think about what you needed from me. I served a purpose in your life, and that purpose is over now."

"How can you say all this? I risked my relationship for you."

"That's not my fault. I never told you to do that."

"Oh, and you're just completely innocent? You never crossed any lines?" I sputter.

"Tell me what lines I crossed. Like, I said, I think you read something into nothing. I get it, you're bored. I'm flattered, kind of. But just reading through all your posts, you make it into something it's not. Something it wasn't. We're just two people who ended up being across the street from each other in a really weird time period, when we're both stuck at home."

"You said it was destiny!"

She throws her hands up. "I mean, it was. It was destined that we'd be across the street from each other, and we were. It happened. Destiny doesn't mean romance. It means things happened the way they were supposed to. That's all. Don't mistake physical proximity for anything other than that."

"But you made me feel special," I say, wiping at the tears I can't keep in my eyes any longer.

"No, Claire," she says. "You made yourself feel special. Don't tell me you didn't love all the attention your posts got, going viral." She finally looks at the screen, looks at me, but I'm looking at someone I've never talked to before. She's suddenly a stranger.

"What are you talking about?" I say, more confused than ever.

She goes on, "I can't control how you feel about yourself. I can't control how you feel about anything. I can only help you think about things differently. Approach things from a different way."

"What kind of New Agey crap is that?" I choke out, tears streaming down my face.

"Look, I'm sorry for making you upset. I'm sorry you read into something that wasn't there. You should be happy I'm not mad at you for putting my personal business all over the Internet like that."

"Right, because you don't believe in secrets," I say bitterly.

"Maybe you should take a look in the mirror. Take a look at the secrets you're keeping."

"But I was real with you!" I say. "In a way I've never been before."

"You didn't even tell me you had a girlfriend. How real do you think you're being?" Sadie looks bored again.

"You always tell me to be true to myself, not be afraid, but you know what? I think you're the scared one. You're the coward! You're pushing me away. That's what you're doing! It has to be!" I say desperately.

Sadie looks at me sympathetically, but not in a kind way. Like, she truly feels sorry for me. Like, I'm so beneath her she feels bad for me.

I'm crying too hard to say anything else.

"I can see you're really upset, so I think I'm going to let you go. See you around sometime when this is all over, maybe? Take care."

And then, she's gone.

And then, I finally let out the big, gasping sob I've been holding in.

I'm not even sure what I'm the saddest about. There are just too many things to choose from. How wrongly I interpreted my friendship with Sadie? Vanessa being mad at me? Hurt, because of me? Being in a pandemic, with no end in sight?

I bury my head in my pillow, getting tears and snot everywhere. I think about how I talked about ugly-crying with Sadie, and it just makes me cry more.

I can't believe how wrong I've been about so many things. About Sadie. How I might have let some stupid fantasy about her ruin my relationship with Vanessa.

I open up Babble. I need to say something. Anything.

But I have writer's block. I don't even know where to begin.

35

Posted by Clarissareads:

I'm going to be taking a short hiatus from my posts. I need to regroup. Appearances can be deceiving. I just need some time to focus on life. Real life.

My girlfriend.

Likes: 2,376

Comments: 513

36

I stare out my window. Sadie isn't on her fire escape. Her curtain in her room is closed. I close my curtain too. I want to forget she ever existed.

I pick up my phone. Not to look at Babble, write anything else on Babble. I open my texts.

Claire:

Can I just explain myself a little bit more please?

I don't expect a response. I don't deserve a response. But I get one almost immediately.

Vanessa:

You have one more chance.

I take a deep breath and call Vanessa.

"I'm so sorry, Vanessa," I say, crying, as soon as I see her face on the screen.

"I absolutely refuse to feel sorry for you! You brought this upon yourself."

"I know," I whisper. I look right into her eyes, those blue, blue eyes. "I'm so sorry. The truth is—"

"No, I don't want to hear it!" she snaps. "You lied to me. You never even mentioned that you had a girlfriend in the posts! You never even mentioned me! You made me feel invisible. Nonexistent. Don't you think things are hard enough for me as it is? Hard enough for everyone right now? Do you even want to be with me?"

"Yes, of course I do. I love you," I say automatically.

"Your posts do nothing to prove that. If anything, it's the exact opposite. Your posts are all about someone else. Someone who is not me. Ever hear that expression about actions speaking louder than words? And ever hear of emotional cheating?"

"Is . . . is that what happened?" I ask.

"I don't know, you tell me."

"I didn't realize what I was doing," I say. "I didn't realize how hard it would be. How hard all of this would be. Lockdown, college applications, life, money things. My mom lost her job, and I'm so worried I won't even be able to go to college at all."

"Claire, why didn't you just tell me about your mom? Do you know how much it sucked to read about it on your Babble posts and act like I didn't know? Act like my feelings weren't hurt because you were keeping this big thing to yourself?"

"Oh god, I'm so sorry about that too. I knew a lot of people were reading the posts, but it still didn't seem real somehow. Like, it wasn't real people or something. And I guess I just didn't want to think about

267

my mom's job, talk about it with you. It would have made it too real somehow."

"Well, now that you've finally told me, and I don't have to pretend that I don't know, I can ask you—is your mom okay? Even if I'm mad at you right now, I still care about your family," she says, crossing her arms.

She still cares about my family, at least. "I don't know," I admit. "She's okay, I mean, she's got freelance . . ."

"That's good. That's really good."

"Yeah," I say. We just look at each other across the screen. I look into her blue eyes, remember how blue they were when I saw them the other day on our date. How Vanessa marched ahead, so sure of herself, of where she was going, even in a pandemic.

"You have everything so figured out," I finally say. "You know where you want to go to college. You know what you want to major in, what you want to study in college, what you want to do after college. I'm lucky if I can figure out what I want to wear each day. Trying to figure out where I want to apply to college, if there will even be enough money, what I want to study, what kind of job I think I'll want for the next like fifty years? It scares the crap out of me!"

Vanessa throws back her head and laughs. "You think it doesn't freak me out too? Trying to figure all of this stuff out? And what the virus is doing to people? How long we might be in lockdown? Everything?"

"No," I answer honestly. "You never seem freaked out about anything."

Vanessa looks surprised. "Really? Are you joking? Why do you I think I've made every single trending Pinterest dessert? Made lists of documentaries I want to watch? Then alphabetized the list? Then reorganized the list based on when the documentary came out? Then reorganized it again based on where it was filmed?"

"Because you're perfect!" I sputter.

"No! Because I am so scared of this virus and what it's capable of. Because I am so scared of life and what it's capable of. And because I know if I stop baking or alphabetizing or making lists, I'll be forced to embrace my fears, embrace my uncertainties. Not just about this virus. About life. About my path in it. About my future. And that uncertainty? That scares me more than the virus sometimes."

"It does?" I ask slowly.

"Of course it does!" she says, exasperated.

"But you've been so calm all along. You were calm that day at school, the day we found out about school being closed the rest of the year—"

"Yeah, and do you know why?"

"No," I say.

"Because I could tell you were freaking out. You were upset. I was trying to be calm. For you, Claire. Because I love you."

"Oh," I say quietly.

"And do you know why I've been after you about figuring out where you want to go to college?"

"Because you love me?" I ask weakly.

"Yes!" she shouts. "Because I love you. I care about you. I want you to make good choices that will make you happy in life. I want you to have a happy life. Because I love you."

"Oh," I say again. Vanessa is quiet, looking at me.

Finally, she asks, "How much time did you spend on these posts? Talking to Sadie? Thinking about your posts, writing them?"

"I don't know. Maybe an hour or two a day?"

"An hour or two a day?"

"Yeah," I say carefully.

"You realize we talked about how that's how much time you should spend thinking about colleges to apply to, right? We said just do an hour or two a day researching schools, right? And you've spent that time fantasizing about another girl. Having some sort of emotional affair or something."

"It wasn't like that. I swear. She didn't even like me. I was wrong about her. It was nothing. It wasn't real."

"I don't care about how she feels about you, Claire. I want to know—did you like her?"

I think about it, really think about it. Think about our texts, our conversations, my Babble posts, then about the way she looked at me in the grocery store, the conversation we just had, the way the fantasy didn't align with the reality. "No," I finally say. "Clarissa liked Sadie. The made-up Sadie. And I liked writing about it. Somewhere along the way it got confusing as people started to read the posts, but it wasn't me. It wasn't the real her. The real Sadie. I don't know the real Sadie. But I don't care. I only want to know the real you. You. Be with you. Can you forgive me?"

"I don't know," she says, and that's when I start to lose it.

"I mean, you violated my trust. Big-time," she continues.

"Vanessa, I would never—"

"It might take some time for me to trust you again."

"I know," I say quietly.

"It may take some time, but, well, we sure have a lot of that right now, don't we?" she asks, exhaling hard.

I crack a smile. "We do," I say. "I'm so sorry. For the dumb Sadie posts, for not being more honest with you from the beginning. For . . . everything."

Vanessa looks at me. "Well, go on." She's smiling.

"Even though we've been dating for six months, your eyes still make me melt. And seeing you in person, even if we were in masks, was hard, but also just so good. I should have said that by now. I'm going to get better at communicating. Not hiding."

Vanessa's smile is huge now. "I'm not stopping you. Carry on."

I exhale hard. "And I'm sorry I suck at figuring-out-college stuff."

She laughs. "Yeah, you're pretty bad at it."

"What if we get in different places?" I ask. "Okay, here is me communicating—I guess I thought the reason you wanted to know where I was applying was because you wanted me to go to the same place as you. That you'd be mad if we applied and got in different places."

I worry Vanessa is going to laugh, but she just looks sad. "Oh, Claire," she says quietly.

"Oh god, I'm sorry," I say quickly. "I shouldn't have said that!"

"No, don't apologize. Not for that. I'm sorry I wasn't clearer about why I wanted you to figure out school stuff. Sometimes I forget you're not inside my brain. Of course it'd be awesome if we end up going to the same college, but, well, I'm making my plans, and you can make yours, and we'll just have to see."

"That sounds like a good plan," I say.

"A perfect plan."

"Perfectly imperfect," I say, smiling.

"Claire, another thing too," Vanessa says. "Just because I think I have this stuff figured out for now, where I want to go to college, what I want to study, it still doesn't stop me from constantly second-guessing what I've decided, the plans I made."

"Really?" I ask, surprised.

"Really. The thing that gets me through is knowing I can always make another plan."

"Make another plan?" I echo.

"Sure! A backup plan to a backup plan. That way, there is always something else to fall back on."

"But how do you know if a backup plan is a good one?"

"That's just it. You don't. But you also will never know if it's a good plan until you try it."

"So you're saying you really don't have everything all figured out?" I ask.

"Yes, that's exactly what I'm saying."

"But you seem so sure of your plans."

"Yeah, because they're plans. Just . . . plans."

"Just plans," I echo slowly.

We look at each other. "Perfectly imperfect plans," we say together.

"You and me aren't so different after all," I say.

"I know. Why do you think I wanted to date you?" Vanessa says, grinning.

"Because we spent so much time together and it was easy and logical?"

Vanessa rolls her eyes. "And why do you think spending time together was easy?"

I shrug. Then I say, "Oh. So did you want to date me because I'm easy to be with, or I am easy to be with because you're dating me?" I dramatically scratch my head.

Vanessa grins at me again, and I can't help but smile back.

"Being with you makes me less afraid. Of the virus. Of whatever is in our perfectly imperfect future," I say.

"You too, babe," Vanessa says quietly.

"So you think we're going to be okay?" I ask nervously.

"Yes. No. I don't know. What is okay right now, even? Like what does okay mean in a pandemic? Does okay mean only five thousand people die instead of five hundred thousand?"

"Maybe we shouldn't try to quantify 'okay' right now," I suggest gently.

She smiles sadly. "You're right."

We look at each other some more, and then there is a knock on my door.

"Claire, can I talk to you?" my mom asks.

Vanessa hears the knock too. "I can let you go," she says.

"You sure?" I ask.

"Yeah, all this talking has made me hungry. My mom and Lucy and I are making chocolate chip cookies today."

"One second, Mom!" I say, turning toward my door. "What kind?" I ask, turning back toward my phone. "Sugar-free? Gluten-free? Vegan?"

"Just regular. Dairy, refined sugar, tons of gluten. The recipe is from a bag of chocolate chips."

"Wow," I say. "Really?"

"Really," Vanessa says, smiling. She blows me a kiss. "Talk to you soon."

I blow her a kiss back. "So soon."

She waves and disconnects the call.

"Come in, Mom," I say, turning to my door again.

She opens the door slowly. "I'm sorry, Claire, I didn't know you were on a call with Vanessa."

"It's okay," I say. And then it's like everything catches up with me, and I'm crying all over again.

I fall onto my mom's shoulder. It's a little awkward because I'm so much taller than her now, but also not awkward because she is my mom. She rubs my back just like she did when I was little, and I know I'm getting snot and tears on her shirt, but I don't care, and I know she doesn't either.

When I finally trust myself to breathe without crying, I pull away, taking a deep breath. "I made such a mess of things. I almost lost Vanessa. I need to make it up to her, show her much I love her. Show her how important she is to me."

My mom looks confused, so I take another deep breath, and I tell her about Babble, about the posts, about Sadie, about how wrong I was about her.

When I've finished, my mom is quiet, taking it all in. "He was right."

"Huh?" I ask.

"You wrote those posts. I can't believe it! Your dad told me about them. He found them in one of those viral lists. Did I use the word *viral* right?"

I laugh. "Yes, Mom. So wait, you guys read all the posts?"

She looks a little guilty. "Well, he did. If I'd known you'd written them, I would have read all of them! It's funny, your dad actually joked at one point how it'd be hilarious if you were the one writing the posts. I told him that he was being silly, that you have Vanessa."

My mind is reeling. "Dad read all my posts?" I rub my forehead. "I can't wait to hear his opinion, his jokes about all this. Maybe he can give me some more dating advice too."

My mom looks surprised. "He'll be so proud of you, honey, when he knows it's you. He's always loved your writing. Your stories."

Now it's my turn to feel surprised. "He does?"

"Of course. We always figured you'd be a writer in some kind of capacity. You've had an active imagination and have loved to tell stories in great detail since you were little. Remember Melvin?"

I give her a blank stare.

"You really don't remember Melvin? He was your imaginary friend from the time you were four until almost eight!"

I comb my memory, but I come up with nothing. "What does this Melvin have to do with anything, anyway?" I ask.

"Oh, your dad was the one who encouraged you to talk about him, tell stories about him. I'll admit, I was kind of weirded out at first, thinking you were talking to a ghost or something. But your dad told you to draw pictures of him, write down the stories you told about him. Your dad has always encouraged and been impressed by your creativity and the stories you tell."

"Oh," I finally say, still trying to remember Melvin, still trying to process my dad as anything but a goofy jokester.

"Anyway, I think you started something that got out of hand. How were you supposed to know the Babble posts would take off the way that they did? We, people, all of us, can be really hard to figure out. Like, why are things like reality TV so popular? Why do things like these dumb challenges exist? Like swallowing a spoonful of cinnamon, why was that ever a thing? And especially now, in the middle of this pandemic, I'm finding people even harder to figure out. People who won't wear masks in public, who won't do something simple to protect themselves or others. Anyway, well, your posts happened to capture everyone's attention. At a time when I think a lot of people are feeling vulnerable and sad. And you know one difference about your posts from all these silly things that go viral?"

"No," I say uncertainly.

"I think what you wrote offered people something."

"It did?"

"Yeah, I think it gave people hope."

"Really?"

"Yeah, really. Everything is so terrible right now, and I think maybe you helped people feel a little less terrible. Gave them something else to think about."

"Terrible," I say, smiling. I think about Sadie and me deciding how terrible things are. Medium terrible, regular. I quickly stop smiling when I realize I'm terrible terrible.

My mom gives me a confused look.

"It's nothing," I say.

Then she looks at me with such kindness I force myself to swallow my tears. "Have you ever been completely wrong about someone? Like, completely misjudged your relationship with someone?"

She quickly says, "Oh, gosh, honey, of course. I think it's part of being human. Trying to figure out relationships, friendships, what they mean to you, what they mean to others. Trying to figure out what's an actual, good connection with someone, and what's a decent connection with someone, all of it."

"Seriously?" I ask, surprised.

"Of course, honey. Did something like that happen with you and Sadie?"

"Yeah, I mean, I thought we had . . . something. Some kind of friendship, some kind of connection. But it's like I made it all up or something? Like it wasn't real?"

"Well, maybe what you had started in reality, then became a fantasy? Became something in your head? You're not the first person in history to get carried away with something, to misinterpret someone's words or actions."

"I just want to forget she ever existed. It was so unfair what I did to Vanessa. I should have told her about Sadie, about my Babble posts, that I was the one writing them, right away. I want to make things better with Vanessa. I need to prove to her that I'm worthy of her. That I love her."

"How do you think you might do that?"

"I don't know," I say, thinking.

"Well, what are some of the things you love about her?"

I take a deep breath. "She's smart. And thoughtful. She tells me what she's thinking. She wants to know what I'm thinking. She supports me, wants me to be the best version of myself. And I just feel so . . . safe with her. Protected."

I pause, thinking. "Other things have been so hard, though. But why? Vanessa is just so . . . good. Like, she's smart, pretty, nice; she makes masks! Like, she's just such a good person. What is wrong with me? Why has everything been so challenging?"

"Honey, there is nothing wrong with you at all. Relationships are hard. They take work. They take communication. And things right now? In a pandemic? They take even more work, more communication. People are scared and uncertain, and everyone is having a lot of big feelings. A few months ago, you could hang out inside together with your girlfriend, go to the movies together, see each other at school. This lockdown is tough. It's tough on long-term relationships, and it's tough on new relationships. We're all changing and not changing. We're stuck and not stuck. Some of us are baking and learning new languages, and others of us can barely get out of bed."

"God, Vanessa bakes so much," I say.

My mom cracks a smile. "She really does. And that's how she's coping. Processing. Keeping a level head. And I think her level-headedness is what balanced you out before this all started. Back when things were normal. But now the whole world has been tipped upside down. Your dad has certainly always been the levelheaded one."

"Dad has a level head?" I ask, surprised. "I thought levelheaded people were serious. Didn't joke all the time, about every single thing."

My mom smiles again. "Okay, maybe not levelheaded exactly. But he's always been able to balance me out."

"Really?" I ask. I can't keep the skepticism out of my voice.

My mom's smile gets bigger. "Yes. Your dad almost always manages to get me to laugh, to smile, when I need it the most. I think I've realized it even more since lockdown started, since I lost my job. Like, when I have these awful interviews over the computer, he'll stand behind my screen, so no one but me sees him, and just do a goofy dance or make a goofy face or something."

"Okay, and?" I ask, waiting for more.

"And that's it! Sometimes that's all it takes to make me feel better. It's the small things like that."

"Hmm," I say, unconvinced.

"I used to think relationships were about being happy one hundred percent of the time, about huge, all-encompassing romantic gestures, about being swept off our feet. But I've realized they're all about the little things. The little moments. Vanessa wanting to watch a movie with you over the computer, Vanessa texting you first thing in the morning, Vanessa encouraging you to work on figuring out your future. Those little things are the things you remember."

"Yeah, my future," I snort.

"What is that supposed to mean, Claire?"

"I mean, what kind of future will I have? Will I be able to go to college?"

"Honey, of course," she says.

"But what about money stuff?"

"I told you not to worry about it."

"Yeah, and you also told me not to worry about the virus, and look how that turned out!" I say more sharply than I mean to.

My mom looks surprised.

"Sorry," I say quickly.

"No, no, you're right," she says. "Dad and I should have been more transparent with you about the virus stuff. I guess we were both in a bit of denial, and we thought that if we just pretended it wasn't a big deal, maybe it wouldn't be one?"

"Oh, like it would just magically disappear?"

"I know, it sounds silly," she says, shaking her head.

"So how is the money stuff any different? Are you going to follow a rainbow and find a pot of gold?"

My mom smirks at me. "Funny. But no. I really mean it, we have things figured out. We have money in savings; I have my freelance. We have health insurance from your dad's job. It's going to be okay. I mean, it gives us a little less money for vacations, but not like we can go anywhere anyway, right?" She laughs loudly.

"So dark, Mom."

She laughs more quietly this time.

"What about my college money?" I finally ask.

"Oh, that's a separate fund. We're not touching it."

"What if there is an emergency?"

"That's what our emergency fund is for."

"Really?"

"Really."

"But you and Dad have been so stressed about money stuff," I say.

"Oh, honey, I'm sorry you've been picking up on any of that. It's not just the money I've been anxious about. It's the uncertainty of freelance.

Trying to keep up my client base, making sure I have enough work. I just really liked the stability of my job before, the routineness of it all, the guarantee. But really, that's something I need to cope with. You don't need to worry about that."

"Nothing is really a guarantee anymore, anyway, is it?"

"Ah, my wise daughter," she says, giving me a hug.

"I've got to make things up with Vanessa," I say. "I can't believe how unfair I was to her."

"You're right; it wasn't fair to Vanessa. Maybe it wasn't all handled in the best way. But, well, you're only a human after all. And you know what all humans do?"

"Please don't tell me it's something to do with the bathroom," I say.

"Okay, you've definitely been around your father way too much." My mom laughs. "No, I wasn't going to say that. I was going to say that all humans make mistakes. Especially when they're young. Especially when they're feeling scared." She puts her hands on my hands, squeezes.

I bite my lip to stop myself from crying again. "Thanks, Mom," I say.

"You're welcome, Claire."

"How can I make it better, though? How can I apologize to Vanessa? What am I going to do about these Babble posts, about all these random Internet strangers?"

"I think the same way you got yourself into this situation. With your writing."

I think my mom may be onto something.

We let go of each other's hands and then give each other another hug.

"I'll leave you to it," she says, and then heads out of my room, closing the door behind her.

I sit at my desk. Where it all began. I open up my laptop.

Then I open my curtain again, look out the window at my fire escape, then the one across the street. The fire escape is empty.

I open up Babble and start writing.

37

Hi. It's me. Clarissa. Well, Claire, really. I owe all of you, anyone reading this, a huge apology. First of all, Sadie. There really is a girl across the street who I see on her fire escape. Her name really is Sadie. We really did talk. But turns out a lot was lost in translation or something. Maybe I interpreted things the wrong way. Maybe she made me think I interpreted things the wrong way? Maybe I'll never know, because she's going back to Massachusetts. She just texted me. She found a place where she can quarantine for two weeks, a friend of her mom's or something, like they have an apartment above their garage. So she'll be there, and then she's going to stay in Massachusetts with her mom because they decided not to make the move to the city now. Maybe I'll see her when she visits her aunt or uncle. Or maybe I won't. But really, this post isn't about her, and I really don't think any of these posts were about her. I think they were somehow about me. But I'll come back to that.

I don't know why I did it. Why I started the posts. Well, I mean, why do any of us do the things that we do, ever? And why now, especially, do we do any of the things we're doing? Why are we baking bread and learning new languages and reading and watching movies and eating?

I think it's because we're coping. We're all coping the best that we can. Life is hard enough as it is, and we're all trying to get through it, and now we're all struggling to get by the best that we can. And I guess in my posts I was looking for something that wasn't there? Trying to create a different reality or something. Something else to think about. I guess it got tricky for me that the more I wrote, the more I realized the posts were a good distraction from everything happening. They gave me something else to focus on. Besides the pandemic, and besides other things in life I maybe didn't want to deal with. Like, fights with my girlfriend, fights with my parents, figuring out college stuff, figuring out money for college, figuring out my life. But you know what I realized? You can't write away from your problems. Your problems will always follow you, even into the stories you write.

Because even though the posts were fun to write at first, and it was fun to go viral, it stopped being fun. When you guys started to question if I was real, if Sadie was real. And when I realized I want to deal with my issues honestly. No more running away. No more writing.

And, the more I wrote about the girl on the fire escape, the more I realized I missed my own girl. My girlfriend. I never mentioned her in the posts because she exists in a different world. The before world. The world with no virus. The world that hasn't been turned upside down.

I didn't mean to hurt anyone. I didn't mean for this all to get so complicated. I'm so sorry, Vanessa. We have such a good relationship, and if it hadn't been for lockdown, I don't think things would have gotten so hard. But it did. They did. I'm sorry. I'm sorry I'm not better at being in lockdown, that I thought we were in some competition that existed only in my head. A competition that I thought I was losing. I had no idea how hard everything would be. I'm sorry. I'm sorry I wasn't more honest about my needs, my wants. You're right that it's up to me to figure out what I want and need and tell others what I want and need. I'm sorry I didn't figure that out on my own, but I can't thank you enough for teaching me that valuable lesson.

I'm sorry for always saying I'm sorry. I'm sorry for writing these posts. I'm sorry for not telling you I was the one writing them. I'm sorry for not telling you how I felt about you. I may have been dishonest in my posts, but I was never dishonest with you. You're better than any fantasy I could have written. You are a million times better than any character I could have created. You're smart, you're funny, you push me when I need pushing, you protect me when I need protecting, and I've never felt as safe with anyone as I have with you. I've never felt the way with someone that I do with you.

Sadie, I'm sorry I misunderstood things. But thank you for making me see myself, understand myself.

Maybe I'll catch you on the flip side. Maybe not.

This picture is me. My hair is a mess. I have eyeliner smudged under my eyes from crying. There's an old pasta sauce stain on my old baggy shirt. One of my eyes looks bigger than the other, and I haven't plucked my eyebrows in a while, and I notice that my lips are chapped. But it's me. I'm not adding any filter. It's me, Claire. And I'm in love with my girlfriend. I can't wait to see her face-to-face again. In the meantime, even if we can't be close physically, I'm going to make sure there isn't any other kind of distance between us. No more hiding behind fictional posts online. No matter how hard things get.

I'm going to get back to why I started my Babble account in the first place, to read and write about books. And if you have a problem with that, you don't have to read what I write. If you have a problem with that, maybe think about what you're running away from, what truth you're avoiding. Think about it. And write about it.

Likes: 64,103

Comments: 13,570

38

I close my laptop, get up from my desk. I look across the street again, but no one is there.

I go out into the living room. My parents are on the couch, my mom with her laptop open. My dad is leaning over her shoulder, reading something on the screen. They look up at me. "Oh, Claire, it's beautiful," my mom says.

I must look confused because my dad says, "Your writing." He's smiling, but rubbing his eyes really hard. "It really is."

"We're so proud of you," my mom says, the tears forming in her eyes. For once I don't try to make her stop crying.

I give both of them a hug and then take a long shower.

My tears mix with the water, and I let them disappear down the drain.

After I'm dressed, I go back to my room with a bowl of beans and rice that my dad made. I don't check my Babble post or my emails. I pick up a paperback, start reading. Might as well get started on some more reviews, get back to why I started my Babble account in the first place.

I'm about fifty pages in when my phone vibrates with a text. I smile seeing Vanessa's name on my screen.

Vanessa:

Look outside.

I'm confused, but I do what she says. She's under my window, on the sidewalk below. She's got a mask on. She waves to me, then holds up a big piece of paper. There is an *M* drawn on it.

I'm still confused, but then she holds up a pen and another piece of paper, and I realize she wants me to write down the letter *M*. So I do.

She gives me a thumbs-up, then writes another letter. *E.*

I write it down, and then she picks up another piece of paper. Another *F.*

I wonder if she's made a mistake, but she gestures at me to write, so I do.

The next letter is *T.*

Meet.

Another piece of paper, another letter. Another *M.* Then an *E.*

I worry again if she has made a mistake, until she writes the next letter. *D.*

Then, *O, W, N, S, T, A, I, R, S.*

Oh my god. I look at her face, what I can see of her face, wondering if this is some kind of joke. Maybe it's one of those jokes that is going to go viral on social media. *Girl thinks she is about to see her girlfriend face-to-face for only the second time in over a month, but wait until you see what happens next.* Then I'll go downstairs, and people will dump freezing-cold water on me or throw something at me. I really don't want to go viral again.

She looks at me, and I decide it's worth the risk. If I'm about to see her in person, not through a video screen, it's worth whatever awful thing might actually happen instead. She waves, and even though I can't see her mouth, I know that she's smiling.

I run out of my room, grab my mask from the kitchen counter. My parents are in the living room. "Can I go outside?" I ask quickly. "I'll wear my mask. I'll stay six feet apart. Please! It's an emergency!"

"Is everything okay?" my mom asks, looking worried.

"Melissa, everything is fine. Her girlfriend is here to see her," my dad says.

My mom and I both turn to him, both of us unable to say anything.

He laughs looking at our surprised faces. "Don't you remember our father-daughter talk, Claire? Your old man knows a thing or two about romance." He stretches, putting his hands behind his head, looking proud of himself. There is a hole in the armpit of his shirt.

"Okay, I also looked outside and saw Vanessa," he adds.

My mom and I are both still speechless.

"Get out there!" my dad says, waving me toward the door.

"Right, okay," I say. My mind is still reeling, but I focus. My girl-friend is outside. Downstairs!

"Good luck!" my dad says as I pull my mask on.

"Be careful!" my mom says, still looking confused.

"Listen to your mother," my dad says, back to looking at his phone.

I run down the stairs as fast as I can, then open the front door of my building. She's there. Standing six feet away from my front stoop. I walk down my stoop steps and then stop and look at her. Not from over a screen.

Her eyes are so blue. I know that from video chats; I remember that from before, but the color is so totally different in real life now. Face-to-face. Because that's where we are. Face-to-face. Six feet apart.

"Hi," she says.

"Hi," I say back.

Acknowledgments

Turns out writing a book during a pandemic is hard. Turns out doing anything during a pandemic is hard. It was therapeutic and challenging and emotional to write about a family trying to get through a pandemic while my family and I also tried to get through a pandemic. I have endless gratitude for everyone at Scholastic, most importantly my editor, Orlando Dos Reis. Thank you for helping me take this book down paths I never would have thought of, asking questions I never would have thought of, helping me think about things I never would have thought of, and considering this book from angles I never would have thought of. And most of all, thank you for your extreme patience and kindness throughout all the revising, emails, and phone calls. Thank you to Nathan Burton for illustrating Claire and Sadie so perfectly, and to Baily Crawford for designing a book cover I know Claire would love. Thank you also to Cindy Durand, Susan Hom, Jackie Hornberger, Shveta Thakrar, and the production department, especially Caroline Flanagan. Thank you to David Levithan, the sales and marketing and publicity teams, and everyone else at Scholastic who ushered this book along.

Thank you to all the booksellers and librarians for all your hard work inspiring and encouraging readers. And thank you for carrying my book.

This strange and scary time has made me appreciate the support of my family and friends more than I knew was possible, and I received so much love and strength from my family and friends along the way. And I thank you all.

Mila—thank you for your bravery and humor and support during this challenging time. Thank you for letting me write, for "writing" next to me on your pink computer while I wrote on my laptop. For bringing me coffee, for patting my back and telling me, "You can do it, Mama."

Nick—thank you for all the times you told me to get back to writing, that you asked why I wasn't writing. Thank you for playing with Mila, making her laugh harder than anyone else can. Thank you for reading the manuscript, and reading it again. And again.

Mom—thank you for reading so many books to Mila, and for finding endless ways to keep her entertained while I wrote, all over video chats. Cosmo—thank you for checking in with me when you knew I wasn't okay. Greg and Erin—thank you for the texts, the chats, for being my personal publicists. Dawn, Bob, and Natalie—thank you for being emotionally present in our lives, especially Mila's, even when you couldn't be physically present.

To all the friends who helped me get through a pandemic, and helped me get through writing a book during a pandemic, especially Jessie Shaffer, Stephanie Rivers, Chelsea Acree, and Mary Funchion. Thank you for navigating the complexities of friendship among ourselves and our kids, and all the ins and outs of socially distanced outdoor play dates, in all the weather extremes. From sweating in our masks to shivering in our masks while we vented, cried, laughed, and watched our kids play. Thank you. One thing I've been so grateful for during this time is all of you, and all of your kids.

Thank you also to Nico Medina, Billy Merrell, Rudha Kerr, Doug

Lenox, Rachel Losh, Tyler Holzer, Lauren O'Neill-Butler, Autumn Stannard, Heather Persico, Siobhan Glennon, Jen Smith, Molly Kolb, Tricia Callahan, Anna Teten, Lucky Longo, Rita Leduc, Jennifer Meister, Meredith-Lyn Avey, Kellie Porter, Lindsey Keith Cole, for the advice, for staying connected, and for staying real.

Oriane Wilkerson, you are one of the real-life heroes, both in your daily work life, and in my life.

To Mr. Righter—thank you for being like Claire's teacher, and for encouraging me to write.

Just like Claire, I'd be nowhere without my readers. Thank you, to all of you, for picking up this book.

Author's Note

I wrote the first draft of this book in the summer of 2020. We were a few months into the Covid-19 pandemic, but no one realized how bad things were still going to get. As we all know, things got much, much worse, and as I write this note now, in the spring of 2021, the United States has reached a death toll of almost 600,000 people, with a worldwide death toll of over three million. It's been an absolutely devastating time, and writing this book has been my attempt to make sense of it all, not unlike how Claire finds solace in her Babble posts. I hope this book helps readers process what living through a pandemic was like in the same way that it helped me, and in the same way that Claire's Babble posts helped her. I hope by the time this book reaches shelves, much of the darkness will have passed, and things will be brighter for all of us.

About the Author

KATIE CICATELLI-KUC is the author of *Quarantine: A Love Story*. She lives in a book-filled yellow house next to a mountain in New York's Hudson Valley with her husband, daughter, and an ever-growing number of animals. When she's not writing, Katie enjoys hiking, reading, and concocting peanut butter and chocolate desserts. *Going Viral* is her second novel. Follow her online at katiecicatelli.com, or find her on Instagram @katie_cicatelli_writes.